A Professional Lola

A PROFESSIONAL
LOLA

◆ ◆ ◆

and other stories

E.P. Tuazon

Winner of the
2022
Grace Paley Prize
in Short Fiction

 Red Hen Press | *Pasadena, CA*

This book is the Winner of the 2022 Grace Paley Prize in Short Fiction. AWP is a
national, nonprofit organization dedicated to serving American letters, writers,
and programs of writing. AWP's headquarters are at Riverdale Park, Maryland.

Book design by Mark E. Cull

Library of Congress Cataloging-in-Publication Data

Names: Tuazon, E. P., 1986– author.
Title: A professional Lola: and other stories / E.P. Tuazon.
Description: Pasadena, CA: Red Hen Press, 2024.
Identifiers: LCCN 2023040156 (print) | LCCN 2023040157 (ebook) | ISBN
   9781636281186 (paperback) | ISBN 9781636281193 (ebook) | ISBN 978-1-63628-234-3
(library binding)
Subjects: LCSH: Filipino Americans—Fiction. | LCGFT: Short stories.
Classification: LCC PS3620.U24 P76 2024 (print) | LCC PS3620.U24 (ebook)
   | DDC 813/.6—dc23/eng/20231113
LC record available at https://lccn.loc.gov/2023040156
LC ebook record available at https://lccn.loc.gov/2023040157

The National Endowment for the Arts, the Los Angeles County Arts Commission,
the Ahmanson Foundation, the Dwight Stuart Youth Fund, the Max Factor Family
Foundation, the Pasadena Tournament of Roses Foundation, the Pasadena Arts &
Culture Commission and the City of Pasadena Cultural Affairs Division, the City of
Los Angeles Department of Cultural Affairs, the Audrey & Sydney Irmas Charitable
Foundation, the Meta & George Rosenberg Foundation, the Albert and Elaine
Borchard Foundation, the Adams Family Foundation, the Riordan Foundation,
Amazon Literary Partnership, the Sam Francis Foundation, and the Mara W. Breech
Foundation partially support Red Hen Press.

First Edition
Published by Red Hen Press
www.redhen.org

ACKNOWLEDGMENTS

The stories in this collection first appeared in the following publications, sometimes in slightly different form:

3Elements Review: "Promise Me More"; *Five South*: "Professional Lola"; *In Parentheses*: "Frog"; *Mulberry Literary*: "Bellow Below"; *Peatsmoke Journal*: "Blood Magic"; *Prairie Schooner*: "Carabao"; *The Rumpus*: "Barong"; *The Spectacle*: "Far from Home"; *Stoneboat*: "Tiny Dancer"; *Third Point Press*: "The Price of a Miracle"; and *Washington Square Review*: "After Bigfoot."

Contents

A Professional Lola

"Love is eternal, love is bloody, love is fleshy, love is meat."
—Jessica Hagedorn from *The Gangster of Love*

Professional Lola

When my mom told me that we were hiring a professional lola for my nephew's party, I pretended to misunderstand her even though I knew exactly what she meant.

"A clown named Lola?" I said, hoping she had made the more appropriate choice for a five-year-old's birthday celebration.

She shushed me and massaged more salt and lemon into chicken thighs, a habit she hadn't dropped since eating food foraged from the Payatas Dump as a child. Even when they came pumped with antibiotics, sterilized twice, prepackaged and freezer-burned here in the States, *manok* didn't taste safe to her until it was lemon-drenched and salted clean. "*Sus.* A lola! What is wrong with your *tainga*? We will pick her up at nine, *Sabado. Mula sa simbahan!*"

A while back, this strange trend spread through the Filipino community. It started with an ad on TFC. For one hundred dollars an hour, a *propesynal na artista* would come to your house and act like your deceased lola. A woman put on makeup in the mirror and crowned herself with a gray wig while the website and number flashed on the bottom of the screen. They didn't come as anyone else. No one could request a grandma, an abuela, a bubbe, a nonna, or even a nai nai. Just a lola.

I thought it was a joke at first, then friends and relatives started doing it. Pictures of them with "their lolas" staring blankly into the lens, TikToks of others' "lolas" missing the high notes to "their" favorite Sharon Cuneta songs. They looked and sounded like the real deals. Lolas I've only seen in old picture frames, Instagram tributes, and refrigerator magnets were taking on new lives beyond the grave via professional impersonators.

Some said its success was thanks to Facebook. Others, word of mouth and maybe some connection with a casino scheme to get more Filipinos afraid of their own mortality and on the next morning bus to the closest penny slots. Me, I liked to attribute it to the Filipino obsession with resurrection. In San Pedro Cutud, just north of Manila, a man has crucified himself every Easter for the past thirty years. Why would pretending to be someone's lola for a birthday party be any different from pretending to be Jesus to perform the Stations of the Cross? The acts were more divine than they were ridiculous.

However, despite its popularity, my mom was never the

type to get into fads or fake miracles. We were traditional in the way where if it wasn't broke, we didn't fix it, and if someone died, they stayed dead. Whenever the commercial came on, my mother would click her tongue, shake her head, and do the sign of the cross, muttering half a Hail Mary and half a curse. I thought for sure she would never hire one, but there she was, having already paid her four-hundred-dollar contradiction.

"So, which one will it be?" I asked the question while also fishing for a reason.

"Lola Basilia," my mom said, getting under the chicken's skin.

Her mom, Lola Basilia, was everyone's favorite lola. It was the obvious choice, but it didn't answer my real question. "Not Lola Adella?"

"*Sobra!* You know your *tatay* couldn't even stand his own *ina*. What makes you think people would want to see her? *Ay nako!*"

"So. What does she do? Is she going to do magic tricks or make balloon animals?"

"*Ay nako! Hindi ko alam!* It's for the olds. *Tama na*, I'm cooking. Do your homework," she said, waving me off with her frustration and chicken juices. I knew if she was doing it for "the olds"—my uncles, aunties, and anyone else older than them—it was out of her control.

At Lola Basilia's funeral, I did a eulogy that killed. It made the whole family laugh, cry, and remember how great she was. I ended it with the first time she taught me how to eat with my hands. Seven-year-old me saw her eating her *meryenda* of salted shrimp, fermented egg, tomato, and rice, and asked her for some. Our kind, wonderful Lola Basilia scooped a little bit of everything and held it out for me with her bare hands. I took it like someone accepting a love letter or twenty dollars to go to the movies. What was dripping from our fingers was her heart.

Throughout her life, she freely handed her love out to me this way. I didn't even have to ask. Even when I confessed to her what I couldn't confess to my mom, even when I confessed that I was *bakla* for boys and not *malibog* for girls like the rest of her *apos*, she scooped up whatever was on her plate for me, her *balong*, her baby boy. How this professional lola was going to live up to that was beyond my understanding.

Then the day came. We were to pick up Lola Basilia where we usually had: in front of the church by her apartment. I didn't expect her to actually be there. What I expected was an old Filipino woman who never scrounged for food to feed her family, never kept her nephew's secrets, and never smelled so much of baby oil everyone was afraid to light a match around her. What I expected was some shadow of what she was, a cheap imitation at best. But, by some miracle, there she was. From the car window, I saw Lola Basilia slouching in front of the steps to St. Dominic's. She had on her pink knitted cap, her giant sunglasses, her Sulu pearl earrings perched above her red knitted scarf, her faded brown coat that she only kept because she thought it made her look like Jacqueline Kennedy, which she pronounced "Jake-lin Candy," draped over her shoulders, and her Reebok Shaqnosis high-top sneakers my Kuya Bing bought her in the '90s that she never took off. Had I not known already that it was an actress, I might have thought we were picking up a ghost.

I turned to my mom and her mouth was agape, just as surprised as I was. Twice, our van passed her in disbelief. After the second time, we were already a mile away from the church and nearly kept driving when the van abruptly lurched over something in the road. In the jolt, I caught a glimpse of a mattress seemingly unscathed in the rearview mirror. After we ran over it, my mom pulled into a 7-Eleven parking lot to check a rattle it left in the back tires.

"*Sus!*" my mother said and banged on her steering wheel before stepping out to investigate. I rolled down the window and leaned out my side. Other than us, there were just two other cars. Beside a Redbox, a man in a beanie was drinking coffee with another man who was vaping, the green light of his e-cigarette flashing on and off between his inaudible talk and listless tokes.

"It was a mattress! How is it?"

After inspecting her side, she knelt in front of the back wheel of mine. "*Aye*, thanks God. *Hindi ito nasira*. Just plastic."

"Plastic? Nothing important?"

She got up and patted the dirt from her jeans. "*Aye, tiwala sa nanay mo.* Trust, trust, *anak!*"

As she came back around the front of our car, I noticed a man carrying the mattress across the street. It was twice his size and he had trouble keeping it off the ground. On his shirtless back was a tattoo that either read "Free Lunch" or "Franz Liszt."

When my mother returned, I rolled up my window as she started the van again. "What was that?"

"You said it was a mattress."

"No, at the church."

My mother exhaled, as if releasing her spirit to speak for her. She pulled out and signaled to get back on the street before she replied, "Lola Basilia."

"Yeah, but how? Where did she get that stuff?" I watched what was left of the man and the mattress disappear in the rearview mirror as we continued back. By then, he had already resigned himself to dragging it.

"The olds gave it to them. We did a surbay."

"Sorbet?"

"*Anak, na naman!* Sir-bay! We answered a questionnaire and gave them some of her things. *Ang kanyang damit at lar-awan at pabango.*"

"You even gave Lola's perfume? Isn't that a little too much?"

"*Ay nako!* Stop now, please. *Umalis na tayo!*"

"I hope they return her things after this."

"*Ako rin*," my mother said, hugging the wheel like the man hugged the mattress.

When we returned to Lola Basilia, she was still there as if frozen in time. We pulled the van up in front of her and she proceeded to wobble her way to the door. She even struggled with the latch like the real her. After a few seconds of watching her struggle, I came out to open it and was met with her frail embrace. I was surprised to smell a hint of her baby oil on her neck mingling with her Tommy Hilfiger perfume.

The professional lola breathed in my hair deeply and said, "*Mm, mabango!*" like Lola Basilia always did. She was good. One-hundred-dollars-an-hour good.

I pulled the latch and the automatic door slid open as its chime started. She gripped my arms as I helped her climb in, then she let go and rubbed her legs as the door began to slowly close between us. My mom examined her quietly as the ringing died. "*Aye, masakit ang paa,*" we heard the professional lola moan in Lola Basilia's voice.

When I got back in, we started off to the party.

"*Kamusta na, nanay?* Long time no see," my mom said, her eyes still evaluating her in the rearview mirror.

The professional lola took off her sunglasses and suddenly looked a lot less like Lola Basilia. In fact, she appeared much younger: closer to my mom's age than my lola's. To my surprise, this discovery left me feeling a little disappointed. Nevertheless, the act continued.

In Lola Basilia's voice, the professional lola told my mom that she had a dream that Lolo was calling her to heaven. She often recounted the same story while she was alive. "*Umuwi, mahal. Sinabi ko sa kanya, mamaya, mahal, mamaya.*"

"Lolo's calling her home," my mom translated. "She says she'll be back later, *mamaya na.*"

The professional lola nodded and put on her sunglasses. Lola Basilia leaned her head on the window like I had seen her do so many times. "*Matutulog ako. Konti lang,*" she whispered to herself and drifted off into familiar snores I couldn't imagine anyone learning in acting school. Beside her, I saw seven-year-old me leaned against her warm body, her slow breaths rocking me to sleep. Between where we were and where we would be later, this was one of many things that needed to be done before we started feeling like we were going anywhere, before we started believing anyone could come back.

When we arrived at my Auntie Felly's house, her husband, my Uncle Bong, was outside smoking his American Spirits. As usual, he was in shorts, flip-flops, and one of the many shirts he got on his travels around the world. My Auntie Felly and my Uncle Bong had retired from doing thirty years of custodial work for the local high school. Unlike my mother, they used their retirement money to go on trips overseas instead of the casinos. They'd been to Europe, Japan, Thailand, and Australia, but the one place they hadn't gone was back to the Philippines. My Auntie Felly, my Uncle Bong, and my parents grew up eating from the same dump. Lola Basilia worked hard to keep them alive while the three of them worked hard to get themselves out. There was no way they dreamed of going back.

As we pulled up to the driveway, my Uncle Bong took one last drag from his cigarette before throwing it to the ground and stepping on it. When my mom parked, he waved the smoke away from him and pulled the latch on Lola Basilia's door. As it opened, I read "Some IDIOT went to London and all I got was THIS!" on his shirt while the door chime rang. Somewhere there was a joke I didn't understand.

My mom pulled her key and turned to Lola Basilia to wake her up. "*Nanay, nandito kami.*"

The three of us watched the professional lola stir and wipe drool from her mouth. "*Aye, Salamat,*" Lola Basilia said groggily. She sniffed and suddenly brightened, curling her arms away from my uncle.

"*Nako!* Bong. Smoking, smoking!"

Suddenly, tears welled in my Uncle Bong's eyes. "*Nanay!*" he wailed and hugged the professional lola tightly.

Lola Basilia weakly tried batting him away before surrendering to an embrace. "*Sus! Mabaho!*" she said. She always disliked the smell of cigarettes.

As we got out of the car and the professional lola went into the house, I remembered learning how important it was to only *mano* my elders, but here was Uncle Bong putting his forehead to the hand of someone almost ten years younger. I didn't know whether to be moved or horrified, but before I could decide, my mother walked ahead of us and announced our arrival, way past the point of any decision-making.

Inside, we were greeted by the astonished and jubilant reactions of more than thirty of our relatives. The olds and the young ones alike *mano*ed, kissed, and greeted Lola Basilia. There was laughter, tears, and reverie. She remembered them all. It was an amazing feat for anyone, dead or alive.

In the kitchen, my mom and I found my Auntie Felly nursing a pot of *dinuguan* and chicken adobo. "She's here, *ngayon*?" my Auntie Felly said, sipping the black stewed pig's blood from the *dinuguan* with a *sabow* bowl. She dumped what was left back into the pot then dipped the bowl into the adobo.

"*Oo-oo*." My mom nodded. From the other room, the loud voice of my Uncle Bong followed by his laughter cut through the loud roar of the cooking vent fan.

My Auntie Felly sipped the adobo broth of soy sauce, vinegar, and *paminta* balls before putting it down. She turned off the stove and the fan and listened to the claps and cheers from the other room. "Get Bing from his room and carry these to the other foods. We will start after Lola does the prayer."

I nodded while I went back through the hall. My mom and

Auntie Felly followed after me before they stopped in the living room with the professional lola as I passed. Behind me, I heard my Auntie Felly greet Lola Basilia with a bad joke I didn't understand. Lola Basilia always disliked Auntie Felly's jokes, but she was always expecting them. I could hear our family laugh and the professional lola call her *bastos*. I couldn't tell if she was crying like Uncle Bong had, but I knew, in her own way, she was just as sentimental.

I knocked on my Kuya Bing's door and waited for him to come out. My Kuya Bing was my Auntie Felly and my Uncle Bong's son and my cousin, but he was more than ten years older than me and already way into his thirties. He still lived with his parents, but he had a good paying job working from home as a forensic accountant and saved a lot of money. Other than that, he was always working in his room and hardly came out, except for the occasional family party. He was much more social online than in person, but who wasn't now?

"Almost done," I heard him say through the door. Inside, I could hear the soft rattle of his keyboard.

After more laughter and applause, my Kuya Bing came out with his usual Bluetooth headset in one ear and sunglasses, but to my surprise, he had on a blue suit and tie too. He closed the door behind himself and nearly bumped into me. "You're here already?"

He gave me a hug and I smelled Lola Basilia's Tommy Hilfiger cologne on him. I knew he had been the one to give it to the professional lola. "Wow, Kuya. Going to a wedding?"

"Shut up. Is she here too?"

"Mom?"

"You know who I'm talking about."

The laughter and applause were farther now. "You do the survey too? What was on it?"

"Not much." He started to move down the hall. From behind, he was identical to his father except my Uncle Bong had more hair. All my Kuya Bing had up there was a ratty ponytail above his collar. "Is she good?"

I followed him to the living room. It was empty now except for my Auntie Milagreen asleep on one of the couches. The laughter and everyone else were in the backyard.

"Your mom told us to get the *dinuguan* and adobo from the kitchen and bring it to the dining room."

My Kuya Bing changed directions and started moving toward the kitchen instead of outside. "My sister and Dumbo here yet?"

Dumbo was what my Kuya Bing called our nephew on account of his big ears. "I didn't see them. Probably in the back. I just got here."

We both picked up a pot and headed to where the food was set up in the dining room. In the center of the food table was a giant *lechon* with an apple in its mouth. Patches of its crispy skin were already missing, having been picked off by my Uncle Weng and my Uncle Arthur, as usual. Beside my Auntie Joko's *pancit*, my Auntie Shela's *lumpia shanghai*, and the rice, there were two wicker placemats adorning the spaces meant for the last of today's *ulam*.

After we dropped the pots in their place, my Kuya Bing and I each picked out a *lumpia* and ate it. The succulent pork and shrimp coupled with the crisp and savory crunch of the egg-roll wrapper was gone too soon.

"You get dressed up for Lola?" I mumbled through bites.

My Kuya Bing had already finished his and was picking up another. "Too much?"

"Not really. You look good in it. It *suits* you, Kuya."

"Shut up," he said and ate another *lumpia*.

I finished the rest of mine and wiped my hands. "Isn't it weird? I mean, it's not really Lola out there."

My Kuya Bing munched on his third *lumpia*. "Just enjoy it. You keep thinking that and it'll be a waste. Is she good?"

"I guess," I said, leaning above my Lola Ester's *kutsinta* and my Uncle J's *leche* flan. "Maybe too good."

"Good. I'll go say hello then," he said and resumed his trek to the backyard.

I followed him outside, and everyone had gathered under the gazebo where the professional lola was seated. It wasn't uncommon to find Lola Basilia surrounded by people at a party. Even when the conversation didn't revolve around her, everyone always just wanted her to listen. She had saved so many of the olds from Payatas and the young ones from America with just her ears alone.

In the professional lola's lap was the birthday boy, Dumbo, with his mom—Kuya Bing's *ading*, or sister, my Ate Sunshine—at their side. She was only a couple years older than me but was already a single mother and a fashion designer. Lola Basilia always called her a *Pantasiya Fashionista*. She supported her and my Ate Sunshine's dream, even when she got pregnant and my Auntie Felly and Uncle Bong kicked her out of the house and stopped talking to her for several years. My Ate Sunshine was gorgeous, and no doubt the prettiest one of the entire family.

The professional lola was playing an old game with our nephew that Lola Basilia had once played with all of us when we were little. She held her two fists before us and asked us to pick between them. One of them had money in it, the other, nothing. "Cat or dog?" or "Dog or cat?" she would say, although we never knew which fist was the cat and which one was the dog, which one had something and which one didn't. Regardless, she always let us pick until we all had something. It didn't matter how many times we tried.

"Cat or dog?" she said with her fists under Dumbo's chin. Dumbo picked one but there was nothing, so the professional lola shuffled them again behind her head just like Lola Basilia. For a moment, I wondered who had told her how to do this, but I suspected it was Ate Sunshine based on the way she watched Lola Basilia without breathing or blinking, how her leg shook in anticipation like when she was the one choosing as a child.

"Dog or cat?" she said with her fists under Dumbo's chin again. Dumbo picked the same hand and there was a folded twenty-dollar bill inside. Dumbo hungrily unraveled it and showed it to his mom before hugging the professional lola. The family cheered and applauded. I turned to my Kuya Bing and asked if he remembered the game, but he was sweating and clapping too hard to notice me.

"Wonderful, Lola!" he cheered and made his way through the family to get to where she was.

Dumbo jumped off the professional lola's lap and hugged Kuya Bing's knees. "Uncle Bing-Bing!" he exclaimed, dropping the twenty-dollar bill on the ground. My Kuya Bing ruffled Dumbo's hair but was still focused on Lola Basilia.

"Ha-how are you, Lo-Lola?" my Kuya Bing stuttered. He kept his hand on Dumbo's head. My Ate Sunshine got up and picked up the bill from the ground.

The professional lola got up and smiled. Lola Basilia shook her way to him as Kuya Bing lightly pushed Dumbo to his mother and out of the way. "*Ay nako. Pogi si,* Bing-Bing!" she told him, and my Kuya Bing, although twice her size, crumpled into a ball in her arms.

"Lola!" He cried just like his father and everyone cheered.

The rest of the night went along with more of the same.

Lola Basilia did the dinner prayer with my Auntie Felly, piled rice on Dumbo's plate, sang "Ebony and Ivory" with my Uncle Rodney, and won at mahjong and Pusoy against my Uncle Roland, my Uncle Bong, my Auntie Lucy, my Auntie Milagreen, and my Lolo Jack. Everyone had their turn with her. Everyone had Lola back for a few minutes. Before we knew it, my Ate Sunshine and Dumbo were already saying goodbye.

I walked them to her car as she carried my sleeping nephew in her arms. The birthday party was still going and there was still an hour left to the professional lola's contract, but Dumbo could never stand being with many people for too long, and when he was tired that meant it was time for them to go home.

"It sucks you gotta go," I said as my Ate Sunshine fastened Dumbo into his car seat.

"It's ok. We'll hang some other time. Maybe during your summer vacation," she whispered and softly closed the door before Dumbo. "You still have to tell me about the boys."

"What boys?" I said, but there had been one on my mind I hadn't thought about since Lola Basilia came back in my life.

"*Sus.* Lola would always ask me, '*May boyfriend ka ba?*' I sound just like her now. Your mom know yet?"

"Know what?" I said, trying to play dumb whenever someone asked, even though everyone knew I was *bakla* except, somehow, my mom.

"*Aye, susmariosep!*" my Ate Sunshine said, staring at the stars.

We leaned on the hood of her car looking at her parent's house, the sounds of our family reaching out to us in the dark. "You think that lola in there is just like her?"

My Ate Sunshine looked at me. "Probably the closest thing to the real thing, maybe."

"Yeah, she's too good. Did you do the survey?"

"Yeah. You?"

"Mom did, but I didn't. She didn't tell me she was getting one until after she did it."

"Are you mad?"

I thought of her without her sunglasses. The look she made that disappointed me. It was the only other time I felt that way about Lola Basilia besides when she died. "I just wanted a say, you know?"

"Filipino parents, right? *Sus!*"

"Yeah."

My Ate Sunshine reached into her purse and pulled out her phone. After a minute, she held it in front of me. On her screen was a woman I had never seen before. "I found her on IMDb. She's been an actress here in the States for a long time. She played a Chinese princess, an Indian bride, a Latina gang member in a poodle skirt. I don't think she's ever played a Filipino until now."

I looked at her many roles, but in all of them, I couldn't recognize Lola Basilia nor the face she had under her sunglasses. "Are you sure this is her?"

"Positive."

"Wow," I said, genuinely impressed.

"I know. She could've been something, right?"

When it was time for Lola Basilia to leave, the entire family poured out the door after her. My Kuya Bing and my Uncle Bong sobbed at each of her arms as they lead her procession from the door to the van. My mom had already said her goodbyes and was waiting in the driver's seat with the engine running. My Auntie Felly and the other olds stood in a line and waved quietly as she was lifted into her seat.

It all happened so fast, there was no time for me to join my mom in the front, so I took a seat between the crowd and Lola Basilia. While the sliding door slowly closed, everyone cried her name and said goodbye, the door chimes echoing with them as if they were bells accompanying a choir. As we drove off, some even pursued us on the street, including my Kuya Bing with his sunglasses and Bluetooth headset shedding off him as if they were feathers of a flustered flightless bird in chase, but my mom didn't slow down. Neither she nor Lola Basilia looked back. The time was up and nothing else could be done.

During the drive, Lola Basilia and I sat in the back while my mother drove silently into the night. As the landscape quickly changed outside the window, I fought the urge to take in her smells and softness one last time. This was the closest we had been to each other all day, the closest we had been together since her funeral. Shoulder to shoulder with her now, I didn't know whether I wanted to rip off her disguise or rest on her lap. As I wrestled with myself in the dark, the sharp hush of her breath got my attention, but I didn't have time to decide whether it was more like the hiss of a sprinkler or a snake. I thought she was done for the night, but behind her glasses, she was still very much alive.

"*Balong,*" she whispered, "*may boyfriend ka ba?*"

Worried that she might have heard, I immediately shot my eyes to the back of my mom's head before I realized what her question and her knowing meant.

Maybe I worried too much. Maybe, in the matter of myself and this lola, and that lola and my mom, who and what we loved didn't matter as much as who and what we believed in.

We believed in who she was. We believed in her love.

"Not yet," I said, before closing my eyes, holding her one last time, and letting her go.

When we arrived at the church, I no longer had to help Lola Basilia off. The door opened and a stranger departed from our van. As the door chime rang, she bowed to my mom and me and said, "Goodnight, it was a pleasure to be your lola," before the door closed and we went our own ways.

The Second Panaderya Attack

I'm still not sure I made the right choice when I told Jolly about what happened at Ninang's Panaderya. Of course, there is no moral lens you can apply to this situation. Which is to say, the wrong choices can produce the right results, and vice versa. I, myself, have adopted the position that things are very much like what the '94 earthquake taught my parents when they decided to immigrate to this country and put all their savings into a house at its epicenter: regardless of what choice you make, you never know what's going to happen. But sometimes, you can learn hard lessons from the results. Or not.

If you look at it this way, it just so happens that I told Jolly about it. I hadn't planned on bringing it up. I had forgotten all about it. Nothing learned, nothing lost. After the earthquake, my parents lost everything they had in America and had to move back to the Philippines. Thankfully, my parents didn't learn not to come back, otherwise I wouldn't be here.

They put pesos together. My dad ferried politicians and celebrities to and from Manila. My mother served Red Horse and Marlboros at a casino in Tagaytay. They dropped it all to come here again. They put all their eggs in one basket again.

Thankfully, the eggs hatched the second time.

What reminded me of Ninang's Panaderya was an awful need to eat Filipino food. It hit us both just before one in the morning. We had split a submarine sandwich, went about our books in bed—hers, *Ready Player One* by Ernest Cline, mine, an on-and-off-again relationship with Banana Yoshimoto's short story collection, *Lizard*—turned out the lights by ten, and gone to sleep. For some reason, we slipped out of bed at the same moment. Like clouds in the distance, we saw it coming, and by the time we reached the bottom of the stairs, it was a storm of tiny razors tearing at our insides, tugging at our tongues. It was a craving like no other.

The contents of our refrigerator were a joke. On the top shelf was a two-week-old half-gallon of milk. On the middle shelf, a small Tupperware of baked beans I packed for lunch one day and forgot to bring with me. On the bottom shelf, a jar of old pickles and minced garlic. The egg drawer had no eggs. The contents of the freezer and the pantry were not worth mentioning. On the kitchen table, a bowl of weeks-weathered tangerines. With both of us working nine-to-five days, five days a week, there was no time to cook. Let alone anything else.

We had been married only a month, first-generation Filipino Americans and college sweethearts (why can't I remember how long we've known each other?). I was a teacher at the time, and she was always an engineer. That hasn't changed. I was thirty-three, and she was a little younger. Things were always happening. We ate what we could, when we could. Filipino food was the last thing on our minds.

Across the table, my wife laid her chest and face down. Her hair and arms spilled toward me like a pack of black and brown spaghetti fanning out from its box. Looking at her made me think of Filipino spaghetti and the thought only spurred the craving on. I picked up a wrinkly tangerine.

"Want a tangerine?"

Jolly didn't move. "That's not Filipino food."

I tossed the tangerine back into its bowl with the others. The thud of their waxy skin making contact reminded me of the labored smack of boxing gloves. "If we had some spaghetti noodles and banana ketchup, we could have some Filipino spaghetti."

"We don't have those things," she said, her tone sounding more aggravated. She had a knack for making me feel guilty about what we should have but didn't.

"Yeah. We don't have hot dogs either," I said, as if contributing to the list would fill the absences.

"And spaghetti sauce. You can't just eat it with the banana ketchup. It'll get burned in the pan and make the noodles hard and sticky from all the sugar."

"I didn't know you were a cook," I said, expecting her to ignore my attempt to lighten the mood. And, of course, she did.

"I'm not. It's just common sense," she said to the table.

Whenever Jolly points out the absence of things or touts her practical nature, I see the side of her that resonates with mine. It is not that they are the same; on the contrary, it is her very core that is the exact opposite of mine. It has its place one end, and mine on the other. They are to never meet, yet they create harmony. They're like the seasons, or beams on a bridge, or the bars the players control on opposite sides in *Pong*. They work together to sometimes keep the ball rolling. Sometimes holding something up. Sometimes revealing something.

And being hungry for the same thing revealed a daydream to me that described the craving with such clarity it was as if it were a memory.

In the daydream, we are in a house during the '94 earthquake. We are both pinned down by a shelf in our bed. Outside the sliding glass window, it is the Philippines. Inside the house is America, California, Northridge, '94 earthquake. Outside the house was the Philippines, Tarlac, Panaqui, the poor town my parents came from, just a normal day. We are pinned together, holding each other tight, unable to move, scared but resigned to wondering what would happen first:

would the roof collapse or would someone from outside eventually come in and rescue us?

"Can't we just go out and find something?" my wife said, her voice ebbing into my daydream as if she were actually pinned to the bed with me.

"And go where? There's nowhere to go at this hour. Every Filipino place we know is closed right now."

"I've never wanted Filipino food like this in my whole life. I want *kare-kare* with extra tripe and some krispy *sisig silog.*"

"I want some Filipino spaghetti with American cheese melting on top. Or some fancy *palabok*, like it's my birthday."

"I wonder if it has anything to do with being married," she said.

"I'm sure that's part of it," I said, "or maybe not."

While the rumbling in my daydream and my stomach continued, this newfound sense of helplessness I shared with her suddenly felt somewhat familiar. There had only been one other time I had been in this moment, one other time I had hungered for Filipino food so much that it hurt. It wasn't just any Filipino food. It was something specific.

"*Pandesal.*"

"Oohh, I haven't had that since I was a kid."

And so it started.

"Neither have I. I was never a fan of bread, but my parents

used to go out of their way to get a bag of fresh-cooked *pandesal* from this place called Ninang's Panaderya in Eagle Rock. They did it every morning before dropping me at elementary school. It was the fluffiest, softest, chewiest, most buttery-sweet *pandesal* I had ever eaten. For years, we got bread from there. I've never had anything like it since."

"Damn," she said, lifting her head for the first time since she sat down. A line of drool dropped from the left side of her mouth.

"I know. When you grow up eating the best of something, it stops you from eating others of its kind. It was the only *pandesal* I could stomach. I couldn't eat any other bakery's or any of the commercial stuff. It didn't taste the same. It wasn't *pandesal*.

"As I grew older, the trips to the bakery grew less and less until my parents weren't taking me there anymore. I had to go on my own. By then, there were so many other, more convenient places to go for Filipino food, a dozen or so more modern bakeries. Several varieties of *pandesal*. Buko. Ube. Red bean. The only one I wanted, though, was the plain *pandesal* from Ninang's. But there were a couple of problems that kept me from getting it most of the time. It was frustrating."

"You couldn't get it anymore?"

"Well, it was far away and closed super early. I didn't drive in high school, so I had to wake up at five in the morning, take two buses for a couple of hours, and get there before it closed at nine. If I didn't get there on time, I was shit out of luck."

"What about school? You missed school for the bread?"

"It was that good. But, to be fair, I would have missed school for anything those days."

"What a delinquent."

"I was different back then. I didn't get serious about studying until something happened before I graduated. Something happened to me at that bakery."

"Was the bread that good?" Jolly's grin shook in my vision. Under the wobbly roof, the light from the Philippines cut across our chests like rope.

"I told a friend of mine about the bakery. Another Filipino."

"A girlfriend?"

"She was a girl, but it wasn't like that," I said, but only because it didn't get that far. "She really wanted to try the *pandesal* too, so we planned to meet at the bakery to get some. The morning of, we got there right before it closed, but the woman who ran the shop had closed five minutes early. We were so angry and hungry. It was kind of like the same hunger. No, it was exactly the same."

Jolly looked up at me. She repositioned her arms under her chin. "If you couldn't get the *pandesal*, what did you do?"

"Well, we did get the *pandesal*, but . . . It's ridiculous."

"What? What happened?"

"Don't judge me, but I carried a knife with me at the time."

"Jesus. Fuck, did you do what I think you did?"

"Yeah. But once I pulled the knife on the lady and demanded some *pandesal*, the girl ran."

Suddenly, Jolly exploded into a fit of laughter. I had never seen her laugh so hard. Tears and snot and drool mixed with her long black hair, her golden-brown skin. When she was finished, she was still dabbing a tear away from her eye. "What an asshole!"

"I know. She went for the police, of course."

"Of course that bitch did. So you got arrested? Turned over a new leaf after that?"

"No, the baker, she was a weird lady. She sorta knew me because I went there so often. She laughed at the knife and cut me a deal right after the girl ran off."

"A deal?"

"Yeah. She didn't want me to get in trouble but my days of coming to the store were over, that was a given. However, she did let me have all the *pandesal* I could carry that morning, provided that I did something for her."

I looked at Jolly's face. Although the bed was still rumbling, I could tell her expression had changed. "What did she want?"

I leaned forward. "Give me your hand."

"Why?" she said, already putting it out.

I took it and turned it so that the back of her hand was facing me, then I proceeded to touch my forehead to it. "*Mano*."

Jolly quickly snatched her hand away. "She wanted that?"

I laughed and sat up in my chair. "Yeah, that's it."

"Jesus, that made me feel super old. I haven't done that to anyone in so long. Not since I stopped living with my parents. I always did that to my titas and titos and, of course, lola, but I never thought someone would do it to me!"

"Same," I said, looking out the window in the daydream again. There was still no one in sight.

"So what happened after that?" Jolly asked, rubbing the hand I had kissed with my forehead.

"Well, I got as much as I could carry, about four plastic bags full, and left and never returned. I savored every piece until it was gone. It was the last I ever saw of the shop. It folded a couple of years ago. I don't know what happened to the baker."

"And your girlfriend?"

"The girl? She stopped talking to me. The whole thing, the bread and I, we were more trouble than we were worth to her. Who knows what happened to her? You could probably find her on Facebook or something."

Jolly sat in silence for a long while. The imaginary house in my daydream began to groan as it shook, the pressure of the cabinet not letting up. She probably sensed that I wasn't telling her the whole story.

"And after that, you changed?"

"Yeah. I ate the *pandesal*, but it didn't really hit the spot. I wasn't satisfied. I wanted more but the place where I could get it from was no longer accessible. I got depressed. You know how depressed I get about food. I graduated and started taking things seriously, but there was always that something. Always that something missing."

"Maybe that's why you and that girl didn't work out. Maybe it's because of that *mano* you did."

"Maybe. But no one was hurt. I didn't go to jail. I got the bread. We came to a peaceful solution. It doesn't seem like a mistake, although it feels like it was. It's like a curse."

"A curse?"

"Yeah, when I *mano*ed that baker, she put something on me." I saw the cabinet in my daydream still pinning us down in bed. It felt heavier than before.

"And now that something's on both of us?"

I nodded. "Maybe. I don't know. Who knows what makes us feel these things?"

"No, you know. You know exactly what you need to do. Unless you do something about it, it'll keep on affecting you. It will keep on affecting me!"

"You?"

"Yeah, I'm the one this time. I'm the one that'll go to the panaderya with you. I won't run away. We'll rob the shit out of that place!"

"What place? There's no place open right now that sells *pandesal*. We can wait until morning."

"No, it has to be now. We'll find a place."

"How?"

"Don't underestimate the power of your wife and Yelp."

We got into my Corolla and made our way out onto the five toward Los Angeles at three. We picked a panaderya that would be open by the time we got there. According to Google Maps, we would arrive thirty minutes before it opened, giving us time to scout the place and decide on a method of attack. In the passenger seat, Jolly watched YouTube videos on successful robberies. She watched hungrily, focused on absorbing every bit of information on points of entry, escape scenarios, scare tactics, and leaving a clean scene. Piled in the back seat were matching camo-colored hunting rifles whose ammunition had spilled out of their boxes and rolled under the seats when I accelerated onto the on-ramp. Two knitted ski masks and a bag of zip ties were stuffed into the glove compartment. Why my wife had these things, I had no idea. She didn't explain and I didn't ask. Married life was like this, I thought, pushing the car down the empty freeway at ninety miles per hour.

The morning was not even upon us when I felt the cabinet ease its weight. However, whether or not this would work, there was no guarantee it would lift the curse, I thought. The house still shook inside in America, the day was still shining outside in the Philippines, and nobody else could help even if they did find us. And yet, the daydream blended with the night as if it one could easily take the place of the other. In both moments, we were trying to fight something real.

Twice, the police ignored us. There were no roadblocks and the traffic lights never lasted long enough to matter. The bullets rolled and chimed like war bells. The moment was upon us and yet I still doubted myself that anything would come from this. Something would go wrong. Someone would get hurt. A regret would surface and stay with us even more overbearing than what was already pinning us down. Something like someone's life or our own roof. But before I could speak a word of it, we were in the parking lot of the arcade. From where we were, we could see the dim light of the bakery shine through the glass windows of the entranceway.

Methodically, my wife reached behind her and began loading the rifles, a bullet at a time.

"Do you have to load them?"

"I'm not loading them," she said, although she obviously was.

"I never fired a rifle in my life."

"You won't need to."

"What if they have cameras here?"

"I looked it up. They don't."

"You can do that?"

"Yeah."

After she finished, she leaned them butt-up between her legs, while she went for the masks and the zip ties. She tossed a mask in my lap before tucking her hair into the back of her collar and rolling down hers over her face. I put mine on, and I couldn't get my nerves to settle.

"It's itchy."

"You'll get used to it," she said and proceeded to open the door. She carried the two rifles out with her.

"What about the license plates?" I whispered, quietly closing the door after myself.

"We'll be out before anyone will see us. I promise," she said, and held a gun out to me. "Leave your door and the trunk open so we can throw everything in and get out fast."

I felt the weight of my rifle. It was heavy, but not like the cabinet in my daydream.

After setting up the car, Jolly and I waited by the door to the panaderya until someone came to open it. It was earlier than they were supposed to, just fifteen minutes shy of five in the morning. My wife rushed the man with her rifle to his side and her hand on his shoulder. He stood straight, and although he was much taller, Jolly looked like the bigger person.

"Inside!" she shouted, ushering him into the store.

I followed after them, the door ringing closed behind me. Inside, we were immediately enveloped by the sweet smell of baked bread.

"Is there anyone else?"

"The money. Just take it. The register's already open." To my surprise, the man was not Filipino. Instead, upon closer inspection, he was a young kid with a tattoo of Johnny Walker on his neck.

"Is this Tito Boy's Panaderya?" I asked, trying to mask the nervous shake in my voice with a deeper tone.

"It is," he said, looking at me and then not.

Jolly nudged him in the side with the barrel of her rifle again. "Fucker! Are you alone?"

"Y-yes. It's a slow day. No one comes until seven."

Remembering I had a gun in my hand, I pointed it at the kid, feeling my guilt mix with my hunger. "Hey, hands up."

The kid complied. "Oh God, what the fuck."

Jolly squeezed his shoulder. "We're going to the back."

We made our way to the back and there, in all their glory, were racks and trays of freshly baked *pandesal* strewn all over the kitchen. I drooled through the mask so much it created a dark wet puddle where my mouth was.

Jolly pushed the kid toward the *pandesal*. "Start filling some bags with *pandesal*!"

"What?"

"The *pandesal*. Fill as much as you can, fucker!"

The kid looked at us and then our guns before hesitantly picking out some gloves and large paper bags from a counter and starting on the *pandesal*. At first, he shook as he handled each one, as if the next piece would be the last one he picked, but the more he did it, the more it became business as usual, until his body relaxed and he forgot we were two people with masks and guns. By the time he had finished with the bags, he was casually bringing them to our car. It was only when he finished and my wife spoke again that he remembered what was happening. He stood behind the counter, as if broken from a spell, noticing the two rifles aimed at him, his hands shooting up in the air again.

"You got all you need?"

"Shut up, fucker! You don't ever say shit about what happened. Tell them you got hungry. Tell them you forgot to charge. Anything but what actually happened."

The kid nodded.

My wife and I began backing out, but before we left, I needed one more thing. "You know what it means to *mano* someone?"

The kid nodded. "My girlfriend's grandpa. This is his shot—I mean shop! He makes me do it. A sign of respect for elders, right?"

I moved toward him and put down my rifle. I held out my hand over the counter. "Here. Take it."

The kid looked at me and then at Jolly. "He's talking to you. Take his hand and *mano*, fucker."

The kid looked at it then, very carefully, reached one hand under mine and leaned forward, the sweat of his head transferring to the back of my hand. I lifted the rifle and we backed out of the panaderya, got in the car, and rushed off with our prize without even having to use the zip ties.

We drove all the way home but couldn't resist the smell of the *pandesal* enough to go inside before opening the bags. Parked in the driveway, we stuffed ourselves with the fluffy, doughy goodness of the *pandesal* until the craving, that craving that felt like it could go on forever, vanished as the sky flushed with color. All in all, we ate two full bags of *pandesal*, with seven bags to spare. We looked back at them, sitting on top of the rifles and ski masks and then at each other. We were full.

"I'm glad it worked out. But did we really need to do this?" I asked.

Jolly rested her head on my shoulder. I felt her twitch like she did when she was falling asleep. "Maybe not, but aren't you glad we did?" she said before falling into a deep, peaceful, silence.

Back in the metaphorical bed again, the cabinet gone, the shaking stopped, the sun of the outside shining through, I wondered what else would befall our house? I pondered this question as I drifted onward toward sleep, full and far beyond empty.

Tiny Dancer

I met him at the wake of an uncle—a faraway one, the kind you forget you had until a wake—and we got drunk and friendly and a little kissy. This was before I met my husband. Eight years ago, when I was less tired and less guarded. He was in his early twenties and I had just turned thirty. His age did not bother me. On the contrary, I found it endearing. I never had siblings, but the attraction was oddly filial without it getting too weird. The fear most Filipinos have about dating other Filipinos is the risk of being related to them. Our families are huge, after all. Add in the factor of a wake and the idea of flirting was as risky as strolling through a minefield. Nevertheless, he felt like a younger brother to me, and I found that pleasant and attractive. Something refreshing compared to the slew of men I dated who felt so different from me they were practically from another planet.

He part-timed at a Foot Locker to earn a meager keep in West Hills while studying Filipino dance from some famous person whose name I could not pronounce nor remember. Although he found classes fulfilling, they ate into his salary so much he would have to bum food from his relatives and the kindness of whomever possible. His money situation was perilous to say the least, but whatever he could not make on his own, someone else did. That may be just my speculation from the accumulated conversations and "food outings" we shared throughout our friendship, but his charisma and passion was enough to make anyone root for him, or at least buy him a cheeseburger.

Despite his charms, I cannot tell you if he was actually a good dancer or not. I am not a dancer nor an expert of Filipino traditional dances, and in all honesty, I still do not believe anyone can actually make a career out of it. My only experiences with seeing them were on *National Geographic* or at a culture festival or two in college. Sure, it was nice and required some skill and practice to do, but no one could make a living on dancing alone. Surely not dancing like a duck.

Dancing like a duck, you ask? When we met at the wake, he showed me how to dance like a duck.

"Do you know the Itik-Itik?" he asked me, nursing a cup of boxed red wine. Later I would discover he was not much of a drinker.

"The what?" I had had two San Miguels and was on my third, trying to list all the Filipino dances in my head but not coming up with any of their names. "Is that the one with the sticks or the fans?"

"No, that's Tinikling, the one with the sticks. There are many kinds of fan dances."

"Sure," I said, unimpressed. I did not find it appropriate to flirt at a wake, but neither did I hold much personal sentiment for the deceased either.

"The Itik-Itik is based on a duck's movement. It's traditionally done by women, but men can do it too."

"Oh really?" I sipped a third of the beer, trying to decide how far to go: was I going to stay or did I walk away now?

"Here, I'll show you." He gave me his drink and took off his shoes. He wiggled his toes through his black socks. "It's better with bare feet."

Then he did the Itik-Itik. The dance looked exactly as it sounded. Starting with a vault forward with his heel and back into a toe-step, his arms straight out to his sides, tilting up and down with the rhythm of his own mouthing of the words "Itik-Itik," he did it just as he described: he moved like a duck. As if wading into a clearing in the reeds, he danced in place, his arms curled in and flapping in the water, his feet alternating, heel out then tippy-toe, heel out then tippy-toe. Itik-Itik, Itik-Itik. All the while, I watched his thoughtful movements and felt the heaviness of his dedication to his craft siphon any bit of judgment or shame I had in watching a grown man dance like a duck.

"You're pretty good," I said, although there was no way for me to truly tell.

"Nah, anyone can do this. But you and me, it's part of our blood, you know?" he said, still dancing. Itik-Itik, Itik-Itik.

"I would never dance that way."

"But you can if you wanted to. And you'd feel good doing it." Itik-Itik, Itik-Itik.

Soon after, we were making out in the parking lot. That is when I started liking him.

We really did not see much of each other after that. Generally, it was once a month. He would call a couple days before and we would go out to a restaurant of my choice. We never made out again, but we had the longest, most intense conversations. We never landed on common topics to talk about, but our interest in one another's differences rallied our words far into many nights. We would leave at closing time after I footed the bill and talk in the parking lot outside his or my car for hours.

Maybe it was because we had just enough differences and similarities, but I had this overwhelming desire to tell him everything. My dreams, my writing, my passing thoughts, my honest thoughts, the things that hurt me, that turn me on and keep me up at night. I never expected an answer or a solution to whatever I said. Just telling him was enough.

Then, a year into knowing each other, his father in the Philippines got ill and he saw this as a sign and an opportunity to explore his roots and to really experience Filipino dance from its source. His teacher, family, and friends gave him their full support. He told me this as I drove him to the airport to send him off. Of everyone he knew, he asked me to do this. I did not ask him why. His father had paid for the whole trip; he was some kind of bigshot in politics over there. I did not put in a dime.

After checking in his bags, we walked over to the TSA line. Beyond the queues, I could see the X-ray machines, the sorting tables, and the empty bins on the rolling belts. It was so early, no one else was there. Just the two of us.

"You really coming back? The way you are, you should just stay there," I teased.

"Yeah, that's impossible. I can't even speak Tagalog," he said, his hand in his jacket pocket, gripping something.

"Walk like a duck, but don't talk like a duck, huh?"

He laughed and let go of whatever he was holding, breaking into a flap. "Quack!" he said and left.

Half a year went by. It was May when I received an email from him. It was June when I drove to the airport to pick him up. The trip had wrung him dry. His features had sunk, the parts that were full now hollow. And beside him was his new girl, whom he presented as a fellow dancer he met in Baguio, his parents' hometown. From the look of her, she was a real poster girl of the Philippines.

She was the same age as him, if not younger, with the unnaturally crisp and bright-colored aura of a freshly cut apple. Her makeup and manner of dress subtly accented her natural swan-like form. A simple white dress tastefully traced her knees. Her nails and toenails were unpolished but flawless. Her hair, a deep black, was tied back and fastened with a classy flower-patterned comb and pin.

The two of them came through the gate holding hands, towing their matching luggage. I was finishing a note on my phone for a story idea when I looked up and saw them. I remember writing the phrase "with every intonation" when I meant to write "intention." I was struggling so much to correct the spell-check as they drew closer to me that I dropped my phone at their feet. The girl elegantly swooped it up like a bird of prey and handed it to me before I had a chance to get up.

It was not a surprise to see her. On the contrary, he had mentioned the girl in his email in May. I thanked her and she took my hand into both of hers. Remembering the way she picked up my phone, I expected her hands to dig into mine like talons, but instead she shook it like a princess from a fairy tale. Like at any moment the birds would chirp our names and we would be whisked away to another world.

Later on, we all went to an In-N-Out. He had been craving an American burger.

"The ones in the Philippines are sweet. I mean, what the hell, right?" he said, lathering a fry in secret sauce.

She and I each had a vanilla milkshake. Not wanting to be rude, I started light conversation with her, but it proved challenging. She mentioned working in the Filipino art scene in Baguio and dancing traditional Igorot mountain dances—her English as clean and concise as her appearance—but no real mention of much else. Instead, she looked out the window at the cars in line, the dimming light above us. He continued to badger me about what I had been up to while I sat there passively responding, thinking of the poor girl. Eventually, he succumbed to jet lag and fell asleep on the table. I called a Lyft for them to his apartment.

"He's always overdoing it, isn't he?" I remarked, shaking my head at his shriveled form.

She looked down at him. Compared to her, we were characters from an old silent film while she was in 4K, singing in surround sound.

When their car arrived, I helped her drag him into the back seat.

"Thank you very much I am very glad to meet you," she said, omitting the punctuation and contractions in her speech, as if her goodbye was merely an exhale.

"Me too," I said and closed the door after them.

For the rest of my knowing him, they were always together. Things between him and I did not change much besides her addition. She did pick up the bill thereafter, though. From what I gathered from his bragging, on top of the Igorot peacekeeper dance and the Sayaw sa Bangko performed on a tiny bench elevated two stories above a stage, she was the daughter of his father's political partner. Born and bred into an old-money hierarchy, she was well-educated and well-financed. Dancing was merely one thing she had mastered.

"What a catch," I dared to say one night while she was in the restroom. We seldom had time alone together anymore.

"Sure," he said, uninterested.

"You're dating a princess! Act more excited!"

"Princess?"

"Yeah, she's pretty, smart, athletic, powerful yet elegant, a dancer—she probably dances better than you, too. Jesus Christ."

"You think so?"

"Yeah. Where she comes from, how can you compete with that?"

"I guess," he moped, hiding his head in his arms on the table as if it might as well be underwater, "but I don't ever see her put in the work. She has her share of secrets though. She disappears on errands I'm not allowed to go with her on. My father and her father's orders. Maybe she puts it in then."

Where she went, we never knew.

Then there was the Sunday on Fourth of July weekend. I was in my apartment staring at a blank screen, trying very hard to figure out the last words to a story before I wrote the first ones—to *the* story I'd spent so much time trying to put together—when he called. I sat by my open sliding door to the balcony, looking out at the early evening. The sporadic sound of fireworks and stench of sulfur filled the foggy air of the neighborhood while I listened to his voice.

"Sorry, we were coming back, and I had an idea: how about we come over to your place and make you dinner?"

Where they were coming back from was a mystery I did not want to entertain, but I did not see any harm in having people over during the holiday. "Sure. I could use the company."

"Great, we'll just pick some things up from Island Pacific and we'll be right over. Probably in an hour."

"I'll let you up. Just let me know when you get here."

I put my story, or lack thereof, away, took a shower, got dressed, and in an hour they arrived. The two appeared to be dressed for a wedding. She was dressed in an elegant yet practical pink gown. Him, a simple black suit. In their arms were all the ingredients for a healthy batch of *kare-kare*. Green beans, squash, oxtail, peanut butter, garlic, tripe—everything came inside. I showed them to the kitchen and where whatever they might need could be found. This was the first time anyone else had been to my home besides my parents.

"We are sorry for intruding in on you like this," she said, already bringing a pot of water to boil. On the table were knives and prepped vegetables. She did this all by herself. She moved with clinical efficiency.

"Get out of here! We got this!" he said, already brushing me over to my living room.

"I can do this," she said, dicing the squash. "You two can catch up. Dinner should be ready in another hour."

With a slow nod, he complied and followed me to my couch.

"So, this is your place," he said, sitting down first and looking around the room.

I sat next to him. There were no pictures hanging on the walls, no trophies or awards on the shelves, no books, and nothing else of merit. Every identifying thing I ever owned was tucked in my closet. I was not one to show off. I could tell he was having a hard time finding something to talk about. "Yes," I said, sitting down next to him but far enough apart for her. "Thanks for coming."

"No, thanks for having us. I hope we didn't interrupt anything."

"No," I started, wanting to mention the writing but deciding not to at the last minute. "I wasn't doing anything."

"Yeah," he smiled glumly, "neither were we."

After an amazing dinner, I poured them each a glass of whiskey, and then one or two more before the conversation lulled and he had the great idea to dance for us.

"Put on something. Anything! I'll see what I can do!" he

said, standing before us, pink from another two fingers of whiskey he had poured himself, eager to perform.

She and I looked up at him and laughed. Her laugh was far more controlled but had a subtle tinge of mischief. There was something there that called to mind the "it" in a game of hide-and-go-seek. I couldn't tell if it was playful or predatory. It was an interesting side to her I had not noticed until then.

I took out my phone and immediately played "The Macarena." I laughed while she quietly watched him do the steps.

"Come on," he said. "This is stupid easy."

Beyond the wall, I heard a firework go off. "Be careful what you wish for," I said and played "Despacito" followed by "My Boo." His body gyrated and contorted to the beat while my lungs ached from laughing so hard. When it was her turn to pick, she picked Filipino songs we were not familiar with, but the dances were just as amusing. He had the ear and the body to move to anything. It was a talent in itself, as far as I could tell. All the while, she watched him, her laughter never swaying from mine.

After an hour and a second encore, he collapsed on the couch. By then, he had stripped down to just his pants for his rendition of Ginuwine's "Pony." She and I clapped for him, although he was already fast asleep. We watched him as I slowly sipped more of my whiskey. As his heavy snores began to lighten and quiet began to fill the room again, I studied her face. There was something delicate and fragile about it that reminded me of a thin veil. When she sipped her whiskey, it was as if something else drank it underneath, something hugging the veil like a hunter hugs reeds in the water, biding their time. After a long moment of silence, as if waiting to make sure he was asleep, she spoke.

"I collect the dancers from music boxes," she said.

"What?" I asked, although I heard her clearly. Her words startled me. She was not looking at me, but her words made it sound like she was.

"Sometimes I snap the dancers out of music boxes." She snapped her fingers with her free hand. Snap. "Yeah. This is very good whiskey."

I nodded.

"There was an embargo on Suntory whiskey last year. Something to do with the lack of supply, or was it taxes? I do not remember, but I spent a year tracking down a good replacement for Hibiki. I may have found it in yours. Too late now, but this is *quite* exceptional. Thank you."

"You're welcome," I said reflexively, although I really meant to ask something. "Say, what was that about the music boxes again?"

"It is not about the boxes. It is about the tiny dancers in them."

"Ok," I corrected myself, as if resubmitting my request to someone else, "can we talk about the dancers?"

"Well, it is simple. I open the box and snap out whatever is put in there to dance to the music. Sometimes it is a ballerina. Sometimes it is a couple. Sometimes it is not a person at all. Like a cat or a rose. Whatever it is. Snap. I take it."

"Ok," I repeated, then paused a moment to compose myself, sorting through the drink to find my words, "why do you do it?"

"Is it weird?"

"I mean, I don't do it. I never met someone who has. I don't know if you're the weird one or if I am."

"That is a funny way to put it." She sipped her whiskey, the veil swaying back and forth with every one of her subtle movements. "I pluck out every dancer I find. I do not care if it is weird."

"Do all these music boxes you pick these dancers from belong to you?"

"Not all of them, no. They do not have to be mine. But I suppose they become mine after the act."

"So you're stealing?"

"Yes, for lack of better words, probably, sometimes."

"And people don't catch you doing this? There are no repercussions for it?"

"How can they? It is quick. I do not wind it up or linger for those that automatically play when they are opened. It is simply open, snap, close. Open, snap, close." Her instructions repeated in my head like the chorus of a song, like the flap of wings. "As for repercussions, people couldn't care less.

Most people who own music boxes seldom open them after the first couple of times. If anything, if they do find out, I give them something in exchange: a reason to care about it again. It is a transaction, not stealing."

"At least that's how you see it."

"Yes," she said with an unwavering smile, her veil light but unmoving, as if it might as well had been a heavy curtain. "That is what really matters. All we ever see. You should know that. This is why I told you."

"Why did you tell me?"

"He told me you were a writer. Writers know how to write what they see. Nothing more, nothing less."

I saw my story peek its head from where I buried it, its words still left to be discovered. "About that, I'm having trouble with it at the moment."

"Do not worry. You will see. You will write." She lightly put her hand on mine. There was something connecting us; something like a thin, unbreakable line you did not notice until you were looking for it.

"Thank you," I said, slowly sliding my hand from hers to cup my whiskey, the warmth of my hand fogging up my glass. "So, if I had a music box, and there was a tiny figure dancing in it, you would snap it out? No remorse?"

She sighed, looking into her drink. "I would feel very guilty, yes. But I would be more remorseful if I did not do it."

"Then it's good I don't have one," I said, not sure of myself and what I owned. It was all piled together in a mess. "And what about him," I pointed, "does he know?"

She smiled, looking at his peacefully removed expression. "Not a clue."

By morning light, they were gone. The last I saw of him was a groggy nod and his figure tipping over and spilling into me, followed by an irregularly prolonged embrace before he left. I felt all his weathered warmth and scruffy youth exude from him like the new morning sun reaching over the hilltop, but I could not tell if it was a simple farewell or something more meaningful. Nevertheless, that was the last I saw of him. Soon after that day, he went back to the Philippines with her and never returned.

That was eight years ago. In that time, the only live dance performance I have seen has been in my dreams. There is one particular dream that reoccurs. Tiny figures fly out of their music boxes and migrate south in hopes of finding dance partners in warmer, brighter climates. By chance, on a trip to the Philippines I took with my husband last year, I happened upon her again in a fancy restaurant in Baguio. She was dining alone when she beckoned my husband and me over. We ate sizzling steaks, drank mango juice, and talked about my dream and what it might mean.

"Unfortunately, I have not been breaking any music boxes

lately. I have a child now, you see. No time. He is at home with the nanny while his mother takes a break."

I did not know why the idea of her having a child seemed hard for me to believe. "That's too bad. I was looking forward to seeing how much your collection has grown."

She smiled, her face unchanged over the years. "Yes, I still think of the one I took from the States fondly."

"You took one from the States? When?"

Her smile widened, revealing the lines of that familiar veil again.

"It was the only one I ever took from another country. It was around the time I was with him."

"The duck." I turned to my husband. "He was the one I told you about. The dancer."

He nodded. He knew all about it.

She picked up her knife, but her plate was empty. "Duck. Dancer. I read your book. I always knew you had it in you. You always had a clear eye for things, people."

"You liked it?"

"I loved it. He always said you would figure it out."

Finally, I built up the nerve to ask her. "How is he, by the way? Do you know where he is?"

But, of course, I already knew the answer. "Who knows? Probably dancing in the sky somewhere." She chuckled into a napkin, hiding her face so well she might as well have been another person. "Dancing was all he lived for, was it not?"

Blood Magic

The Filipina wife sits in the back of the car as it goes. She likes it there, and her American husband does not mind it. He thinks that it makes him look protective. The Filipina wife quips that it makes him look possessive. They laugh. They have not been married for a year yet, but she already smells someone else's perfume on him, notices him say he has been with her in places that she has never been before.

The things outside go by. They are what she understands as America. Traffic. A flush of trees and signs and order. Tall buildings, brush, and then the model homes, one after another, the same but different. She is going to her department chair's model home for their book club. Where he is going, she does not know.

It isn't a normal club. They read and attempt spells from an old library book her department chair found. They are harmless spells written at the turn of the century for wives with too much time on their hands. Her department chair copies pages from the book. She scans and prints them on the school printer. Once, she accidentally left her printouts on the copier and they were found by their principal. Her department chair's excuse was that it was going to be repurposed for an annotation assignment. The principal ate it up. The principal had been one of those teachers who were only in the field for a year. What teachers did was still magic to her. It wasn't a lie. A spell could be a lesson.

The Filipina wife and her department chair are both teachers at a middle school. They both teach English and are both immigrants from the Philippines, although it has been twenty years since her department chair has been back and only two since the American husband petitioned to get his Filipina wife here. Where the Filipina wife saw pristine rice paddies cascade into the glistening steps of Mountain Province, her department chair could only remember burning garbage, their pillars of black smoke reaching for her departing plane.

The Filipina wife wonders how her department chair is able to control her own American husband. Her department chair's husband works from home in forensic accounting, but he is never there when she comes over. She doesn't know where he goes. She sometimes imagines that he is stuffed in a pen like her family used to keep goats. She imagines him blindfolded like her father used to keep them. He explained it was to prevent them from getting hungry and overeating. The thought gives her a weird sort of thrill.

She looks at the back of her American husband's head and imagines him in a pen, blindfolded. She imagines that his eyes are wide open but can't see. She wonders if this makes it easier for her to see what's on his mind. She wonders if she would see her face or another's he is hungry for.

"Baby?" she says. She sees his eyes look at her and then the road. She doesn't have to do anything to know what is there.

"Nothing," she says and looks out the window.

The Filipina wife comes out and her Filipina American friend, Beanie, is dropped off at the same time. Beanie's husband is too big for their car. He used to be a basketball player for the NBA. Beanie is a science teacher at her school, but she doesn't have to be. They have money but she can't have kids. She and her husband mentor kids and invite them to her house instead. Once, the Filipina wife and her American husband visited. She, Beanie, and Beanie's husband played team tennis with their students while her American husband moped on a lawn chair and stared at his phone. They have not gone since.

"You get a Lyft?" Beanie asks.

By then, the Filipina wife's American husband is gone, as if he were never there. She is surprised Beanie noticed. "No, *mabakit*? Why?"

"You came out of the back seat. I was just thinking some-body else was bringing you in."

"*Hindi*, we just do that."

"Just do that? That sounds fun!"

"It is. *Diba?*" she says, but it isn't.

The two get to the door and, before they can ring in, the door opens. Her department chair stands in the door, a fist to her hip, the back of her hand to her forehead. She lets her head back and her long black hair falls. She wears a black blouse with a long fall-colored skirt. Her veiny ankles are exposed between the skirt and her pointed black-buckled shoes.

"Darlings! Welcome back to the coven."

Beanie wipes a tear from laughing too much. "I love you! You're so full of shit!"

They embrace and each give and receive pecks on the cheek.

"Darlings, the only thing I am full of is wine, *talaga!*"

The conversations start mundane, then move to school things. They talk about the kid who was caught with half a scissor the other day. He was sharpening it with the other blade. Did he know what he was doing? Was he really doing anything? They didn't know, but just to be safe, admin fol-lowed the protocol. He was always talking to himself. The Filipina wife remembers watching him go back and forth be-tween a tree and a bench.

During the Halloween Festival, the Filipina wife remembers reading his palm for a ticket. She saw a mind line that went straight across his hand, a small welt in the center dividing one half of the line from the other. His mother was young, blond, and beautiful. She read palms too. She told her son he couldn't run away from his hands. She was wearing scrubs, but the Filipina wife couldn't tell if it was her uniform or a costume.

"I saw his mother," the Filipina wife says. "She was very understanding. *Maawain siya.*"

"Is she a doctor?" her department chair asks, her nose diving into her glass.

"No clue," Beanie says, touching the tips of her fingers. "Would a doctor be able to come in any time she wanted?"

"I don't think so. *Hindi ko alam,*" the Filipina wife says, although she likes to believe that she would be. She thinks of going shopping with her. She thinks of going out to lunch dates with her that would turn into dinners. She thinks of her dying her hair blond. She thinks of them keeping each other's secrets. Why couldn't she make more non-Filipino friends? Why did she only have her American husband and his friends?

They eat. It is a beautiful roast that has been in the Crock-Pot all day with wine and thyme. Her department chair's husband put it in there before he left.

"Oh, he hates this stuff, but he loves to cook it," her department chair says. "He would rather eat fast food somewhere."

The Filipina wife imagines him eating fast food in a pen, her department chair feeding him. She imagines him eating everything, even the wrappers. She cleans her plate at the thought. The others think the Filipina wife is hungry, but the thought of her husband with someone else has been on her mind. She is worried. A man or a woman or a goat, the difference didn't matter.

They crack open the book and go to their next spell. It is a spell to make bad thoughts go away. On the table, there are all sorts of ingredients. The basics include lavender and dried flowers they get from a local holistic dispensary they Yelped. The only thing that looks out of place is the honey. It is generic honey in a plastic bottle shaped like a bear. Most of the spells require them to leave honey outside of the door. Once, they had forgotten about the honey and the Filipina wife thought it would be all right to leave some outside of her classroom the next day. When asked by her students what she was doing, she told them she was using the honey to lure a bee out of the room. This upset a student allergic to bees before the Filipina wife dismissed him to the nurse's office. The rest of the class occasionally looked up at the lights or turned their heads. The idea that they were looking for something that wasn't there amused her, but she could understand their plight. At the end of every spell was an anticipated disappointment, but it was fun to believe in things that didn't happen. It was fun to believe in the unbelievable, even only for a little while.

The spell requires the usual mixture of herbs and dried appendages. There are tails of eight different animals. Legs of six animals and five different insects. There are spider eyes, although they are indistinguishable from ground pepper. Her department chair had dared one of them to taste them, but no one wanted to make the confirmation. The Filipina wife imagines the grate of the eyes on her tongue. She expects to taste what they see. She expects a sour pain. She expects to taste something acidic that would eat her away.

There are jars with pickled things and jars of blood. Last week, a spell had called for goat blood. Her department chair had learned that the best way to collect a goat's blood was to suffocate the goat to death, so she had her husband do it. According to her department chair, he was "such a child about it," but he did it. The Filipina wife knew goats sounded just like human beings when they screamed, but she had never heard one dying before. She tries to imagine the sound the goat made when it was gasping for breath, but she can't even imagine the sound of a human being struggling to breathe. She wonders what sound her department chair's husband made. She wonders if a goat could cry like a child too.

"Saw it on an episode of *No Reservations*," her department chair replies when the Filipina wife asks where she had learned about goats. "Oh, Anthony Bourdain. So sad, you know."

"What happened to him?" Beanie says. She is chewing on a cherry stem. They have fresh cherries that are not part of today's spell but might as well have been.

"Darling, *talaga*! You must be kidding me."

"What? What about him? I really don't know what you're talking about."

"Anthony Bourdain. He's dead. *Aye, patay na.*"

"Oh, wow. When did that happen?"

"I don't know. It happened and it's sad, darling. *Ansabe ko?* A man's dead."

"Sorry."

"Don't say sorry to me," she says and drinks her wine in the silence that follows before she speaks again. It unnerves everyone when she does this, and it happens often. "There isn't anything to do about a dead man, *talaga*. No need to apologize for what's natural. *Diba?* Anyway, the lions."

"Lions? I thought we were talking about goats?"

"No, there were lions in the episode too. This superhuman tribe had been at war with this pride. I think that's what they're called, a group of lions, *a pride*. Anyway, they were at war with this pride for centuries and this American woman—leave it to Americans—comes in with her Jeep and college learning and tied-back hair. She puts her privileged foot down and says they can't kill all the lions. This tribe farms goats. I forgot to mention that. This tribe's primary diet is goats and blood. Goat blood, cow blood, lion blood. It doesn't matter. Any blood will do. They have a diet of only meat and blood.

"The lions, guess what, darlings, the lions also have a meat and blood diet, so they are in constant competition for the meat and blood in their entire world. But this American woman, this know-it-all, comes in and says they *must* coexist. That it's important that the lions are kept in check but not killed. And this tribe had been killing them for centuries. This tribe were lion killers. Lions were afraid of them. And, darlings, these weren't any regular old pussies. These things had teeth. These things could bite. These things could swallow a person whole. Anyway, I don't remember where I was going with this."

"How do the goats play into this?" Beanie slurs, drunk but still paying attention. The cherry stem falls from her mouth to her feet. It points at the Filipina wife like a compass.

"Oh, darling. Forget the goat. The goat is dead. Anthony Bourdain and my husband killed it by choking it to death. Poor man felt terrible about taking its life that way. And now he's dead, too. *Talaga*."

The Filipina wife cannot tell who she is talking about: her husband or Anthony Bourdain. She feels her lungs well with blood. She tries to imagine what it is like to be choked to death. What it feels like to drink someone's blood and get stronger. What it feels like to swallow your own and die.

The Filipina wife knows the taste of goat blood. When her family slaughters a goat, they put the blood in a slow-cooked *papaitan* along with shreds of skin and organs and green peppers. The stew would smell awful until the blood cooked and thickened and sweetened the pot. Before her eyes, the goat transformed. The blood, its magic.

They pick out four spider legs and put them in the concoctions they have in front of them. There is a bar of cinnamon and a cherry stem swimming in the Filipina wife's half-empty cup of Diet Coke. She drops the legs into her cup and watches them make ripples beside the stem. The stem is not supposed to be there, but the others do not correct or notice it. She imagines each of the ingredients communicating with each other. They are sharing a secret in a language only they know. Beanie pinches the cinnamon out of her cup and stirs her brew. She looks like she is concentrating but the Filipina wife knows she is drunk after two glasses. Beanie is always this way. Beanie is always hard on herself. Beanie is always not able to take it.

Her department chair shakes her cup in her hand. She holds it above the spell book and her finger runs over the words. Her department chair is always the one who picks the spells. It is her book and that allows her the right, but she never allows the other two to read it. She always must be the one to see and choose.

"*Susmariosep!* There's a part here about us doing something else, but I don't understand it."

"What does it say?" Beanie leans in, but her department chair's shoulder crowds her path to the book.

"Darling, please, *sandali*. I am trying to read. How can I understand if you won't let me investigate!"

Her department chair leans further in. She nods. The Filipina wife looks into her cup and theirs. They are all different and she cannot tell which one is right. Perhaps they are all wrong. Perhaps they are all right. Beanie continues to stir her potion.

"It says we need to do a joining and relieve the embers to the wind."

"I haven't done that with Richard in a long time. Too long," Beanie jokes and stirs her potion more rigorously.

"Oh darling. *Ganon?* You never know what to keep to yourself. *Diba?*"

"That's what it sounds like, doesn't it?"

"Darling, there is nothing metaphorical in these instructions. It is all literal. Clearly the embers are related to fire. But a *joining*. I just don't know."

The Filipina wife takes out her phone. She searches up "joining" but nothing comes up. Nothing relates to any witchcraft. Everything relates to the sexual connotation of the word. She remembers the last time she and her American husband made love. They had gone on vacation to San Francisco. He had mentioned that, just once, he wanted to sleep with a blond, so she pretended to be one.

The vacation started just like any other vacation. They went sightseeing. They saw the Golden Gate Bridge, they saw the crooked road, they saw all the streets that slouched on the hills in all the impossible ways they couldn't where they were from. This was the aim of their vacations. It wasn't until they went to the hotel that things deviated from the plan. She left their room saying that she was going to get ice but went to their car instead. There, she uncovered a change of clothes she'd hid under the spare tire. She put on sexy lingerie and a trench coat and a blond wig. She went back upstairs, feeling embarrassed as she passed through the lobby. But as she went up the elevator, she began to feel more and more confident. She thought of her background. Her motivations. She thought of the character she was going to play.

By the time she knocked on the door, her name was Sylvia and she had been phoned in for a client. Her husband looked her up and down in shock. She came inside and talked all business. He didn't question what she was doing and went with it. He asked about what services were available. What the costs were. She asked him to take a shower and he did. The control excited her, and she could tell that the lack of it excited him too. At the end of the night, he paid the fee and she left.

Every day of the trip continued like this. They spent the day like a normal couple and went sightseeing. They saw Fisherman's Wharf, they went to a museum, Alamo Square, all the hipster restaurants, Chinatown, bookstores. Then, at night, they would continue their escapade. She was the blond Sylvia, not his Filipino wife, and he loved it. At the end of the vacation, it was worth it to become someone else.

"Maybe the joining means we need to set all of this on fire? *Sunugin ito*," The Filipina wife hears herself suggest, but it is Sylvia's voice that comes out when she says it.

"Darling, how do we set a liquid on fire?"

"There are ways. Maybe we have to boil it down and burn it. *Lutuin mo.* Maybe we're supposed to put out a fire with our spell."

The Filipina wife thinks of her husband. She remembers his face when he heard Sylvia's voice. It wasn't the same face she saw looking at her in the mirror earlier today. It was a different kind of face. She wants to see that face more often, but she can only see the face with someone like Sylvia going down unfamiliar streets. She can only see the face in a dark pen, blindfolded and struggling to breathe.

"Darling, you may be on to something. I'll start a fire in the grill outside and then we'll do it together. We'll pour it in all together like we were touching the tips of our swords like the three musketeers!"

Inside, the Filipina wife watches her department chair get the grill ready outside. She is crumpling pages of a magazine and putting them into the grill. She thinks she sees herself on one of the pages she crushes, but it's not from anything she would ever be in. Beanie is in the bathroom, hugging the toilet.

The Filipina wife made the excuse of having to call her American husband and stayed inside. She put the phone to her ear as her department chair left, but she never dialed. She keeps the phone to her ear and looks down at the book. The spells are in alphabetical order based on the need. She turns the page. There is one for rewinding time. Another for nagging children. There is one just labeled "mothers." Finally, she gets to L. In it, she sees what she is looking for.

The spell asks her to think of who she wants the bond fulfilled with while making the potion. She thinks of her American husband. She thinks of his face when he is thinking of someone else. She thinks of his face while they are sightseeing. His face is in the reflection of a bakery window in Fisherman's Wharf. His eyes are outside of his head. They are floating outside of the holes and beyond the glass. She reaches for them, but they disappear. She thinks of his face when they married, when they first met, when they see each other across a crowded room. His eyes are moving closer to her, but they are looking the opposite direction.

She pulls the tail of a rat and three of the spider eyes. She puts them in a fresh cup. She gets out the jar of goat blood and even with the lid still on the smell almost makes her gag. She holds her breath and quickly opens and closes the jar, pouring it in with the dry ingredients. She wipes the brim dry with her thumb. She lifts her thumb to her nose and coughs. She stirs the cup with another stick of the cinnamon. The last ingredient is her own blood. She picks up a plastic knife from the table and lets its teeth bite into her thumb, the one she used to dry the goat blood. She wonders if she is going to contract some sort of disease. Maybe it will change her? Maybe her hair will change color? Maybe she will put on the face of her husband's mistress?

She tries to imagine what her face looks like as the plastic teeth of the knife bite into her thumb. One stroke and a line of blood appears and drips once into the cup. She lets the drop's red arms stretch across the surface before mixing it with the cinnamon stick. The spider eyes float to the top. She wonders if it is enough. Nothing is ever enough, but she will give more if she has to.

Outside, her department chair is dipping the lighter into the mouth of the grill. She frowns down in displeasure and is not her usual confident self. The Filipina wife flips the book back to where it was before she started and walks into the kitchen. She runs her thumb under the tap until the bleeding stops. She wraps her thumb in a paper towel and squeezes. On the refrigerator, her department chair and her husband smile. She imagines her husband's face over his body. She imagines him choking a goat to death for her. She imagines him choking her department chair, and then his mistress with her face, and then herself. She feels the blood well up in her chest. She feels her heart about to burst.

Outside, she and her department chair hold their cups before the fiery mouth of the grill. The Filipina wife is afraid her department chair will notice the strong smell of the goat blood, but the smell of the coals and burned pages masks everything else. Her department chair looks over the house, her face lit orange by the fire. The light dims. The sky is blood red.

"Where the hell is she, *talaga*?"

The Filipina wife looks inside and sees the open book. It is only then she realizes the inside must smell like goat blood. She thinks of the strong stench and feels the tuck of fear from being caught. But what will be the consequence? If everything worked out, would there still be a need for an apology? If everything ever really came true, what did they really deserve?

Beanie comes out through the side door. She has a cup and her purse on.

"I'm sorry. I got a call from my husband while I was in the bathroom. I have to go."

"Oh no, darling. *Ansabe?* What is this about?"

"He says it's a surprise."

"Oh, a surprise? How vague."

"I know! I wonder what it could be. He's waiting for me already."

"Darling, there's at least another hour before our allotted time. Still more spells to do! Come on, have another drink, he can wait."

"I'm sorry, really, I am." Beanie takes her spot beside the Filipina wife. She imagines Beanie's face on the body of her American husband's mistress. She imagines him choking her to death.

The Filipina wife says, "I forgot to mention, my husband said he was coming too. Sorry *na*."

"Maybe all our husbands are conspiring against us? Maybe they have a spell of their own?" her department chair says. Her face is so removed from the Filipina wife's. It is hard to imagine them coming from the same place.

"Let's finish this spell," Beanie says.

"All right, darlings. Remember, it's like tipping our swords. *Talagang* three musketeers. I'll count. At three, we pour."

Her department chair counts but before she gets to three, the Filipina wife pours hers in. A second after, the others follow. The smoke rises and the smell of the ingredients fumes into the air.

The Filipina wife looks at the smoke. She can smell her potion more than the others. She can feel its power. She sees her American husband turn in the distance. She sees him begin to make his way to her. She sees him follow the smoke.

Barong

It was Christmas Eve, a year after Duterte was elected, when my brother and his family were killed in a shopping mall fire in Davao City, Philippines. His wife and two girls were found in a furniture store; my brother, the food court. Based on the coroner report, he was holding two ice cream cones when he died. He was ten years older and had his own life there, while my parents and I had our own here in America. He was part of my parents' old life and when they left, he stayed behind.

Needless to say, I didn't grow up with him. I was born in America. He was family and my kuya, but he wasn't someone I would talk to other than the occasional "happy birthday" or liked post on Facebook. His death didn't really bother me as much as the idea of the wrappers of the cones being singed to his hands. The thought of them was clearer to me than my brother and his family's faces.

When I told my boss about the hands and asked for a few

days off to attend my brother's funeral, he sighed and suggested I didn't.

"Going over there and doing something like that will just make your dreams worse. Be grateful it's just the hands you think about," he said through the phone. I could hear something sizzle on his side. "If you go, you're just going to regret it. I know you."

At the time, I was still in college and working as the secretary for a small family law office that specialized in cases related to Filipinos and divorce. My boss was just three years older than me but already he had his own practice. We immediately took a liking to each other, and as long as I did what he said, even if I didn't understand it, he promised to take care of me. He was like my kuya, so naturally I told him everything.

"You're probably right," I said, but then insisted, not wanting to disappoint my parents.

"Tell them I said you couldn't." Something on his end bubbled and hissed. "It's my fault."

"Is that your final decision?"

"Your choice."

"Don't shoot the messenger?"

"Exactly," he said to the sound of a plate dropping on a muffled surface.

So, the following week, I stayed in the office and the funeral went on without me. My parents grieved my brother for a year, but they never blamed me for not going. The nightmares about my brother's hands eventually went away. New worries became old ones and, eventually, nothing to worry about at all. My boss said everything came and went like that, all while I took calls, scheduled appointments, and made copies. My life had been reduced to necessity. Nothing more, nothing less.

My boss was an eccentric person, to say the least. He never ate lunch, never appeared stressed, and he was extremely punctual and neat. His appointments always started and ended on time and not one thing in his office was out of place. He made sure everyone's time was respected, everything was given, received, organized, and kept. In this fashion, I learned his pace and adopted it as my own. My stomach stopped rumbling at lunchtime, my stress stretched into obscurity, and I made sure my time and my actions were never wasted.

The most interesting thing about my boss was that he wore a barong every day. There was seldom a time I saw him without one. For our Filipino clients, seeing someone wear a barong in the office was like seeing a politician or a father of the bride, not their divorce lawyer. Upon their first meeting, I would open the door to his office and their eyes would brighten with a sudden air of alarm, as if they had come to the wrong place. My boss would rise from behind his desk, his transparent and elaborately embroidered white barong hugging his form like a coat of mist, and greet them, assuring them they did not make a mistake. For our non-Filipino clients who were not familiar with it, I imagined the exotic nature of the barong in contrast to what they saw underneath—typically a plain white T-shirt, black dress slacks, and black dress shoes—brought to their minds a lowly server in a restaurant rather than a person of power. I have witnessed, time and again, these kinds of clients talk down to him, their respect for him measured by the thickness of what he wore. But he and his barong always won them over. Eventually, these clients saw the barong and my boss for what they were.

Appearance aside, my boss took his work seriously. He kept his paperwork organized, his dates calendared, and his clients educated, informed, and happy. He collaborated with each client to identify and implement the best course of action to meet their desired outcomes—even, at times, giving them more than they knew they were asking for. A client who wanted alimony would get it—and an extra fifty dollars. Visitation? He would give them that and an extra day. The house? Well, my boss offered, how about some renovations, too? There wasn't anything a client asked for that he didn't think deserved a little extra added to it.

And, like some saint, my boss even lived a simple, pious life. He drove a fifteen-year-old Corolla, lived in a one-bedroom apartment in the industrial park close to his practice, and kept miniature rewards cards for several grocery stores on his keyring. As for vices, there were only two I could speak of: his love for vodka martinis and spoon-muddled old-fashioneds. He made one of each whenever I went over to his place, though I only ever wound up there to borrow and return a barong. Always for a wedding. Always the same barong. Always the two drinks. Everyone around me was getting married, while everyone around him was getting divorced.

"I'm sorry to always be doing this to you," I said, accepting a martini from him one night. In it were three pitted green olives. He once explained that even numbers in drinks were always bad luck.

"No problem. You can borrow one whenever." He sat down across from me, the perpetually borrowed barong hanging on the chair next to him like a shadow in a clear plastic shroud. "Whose it this time?"

"A cousin."

"Wasn't it a cousin last time?"

"You know, us Filipinos and our big families. It's a wonder you and I aren't related."

"About that . . ." he joked, and we laughed, each of us spilling a little of our drinks on the table. "Although I wouldn't be surprised. You fit in my barongs."

"Well, I just borrow the one. Besides, aren't they all one-size-fits-all kind of shirts?" I asked.

"Well, some. Most come in the standard small, medium, large. Still, these are special. They're custom-made and fitted by my guy. I didn't think anyone else could wear them, but you fit in one of mine, you fit in them all." He swabbed his spill with his finger and dried it off in his jet-black hair. I looked to do the same to my own mess, but it was already gone.

"I didn't know there was a guy for that," I commented into my drink. The mixture was so clear it looked like the olives were nestled at the bottom of an empty glass. My boss explained that the trick was to stir and not shake. This was real life, he said, not James Bond.

"There's a guy for everything. There's a guy for your fridge, a guy for your water, a guy for your cable. Why can't you get a guy for your barongs?"

"I guess," I conjectured. "Still, barongs. That's a tall order." We sipped our martinis at the same time. The subtle floral notes and clean finish masked the bite.

"My guy's like the *arbularyo* of barongs. Don't ask how. He delivers. You want his email?"

"Oh no. I'm better off borrowing the barong from you. Comes with free drinks."

"Hear, hear!" My boss raised his glass. "And free company."

"And free fucking company!" I raised my glass in reply and took another sip with him, feeling the drink begin to warm my insides. "You know, at the rate these weddings are going, I'll probably be coming over once a week like this. Probably even borrowing more barongs than just the one."

"Good for us, good for business." My boss finished off his drink and got up to start another at his bar.

Not wanting to be left behind, I downed the rest of my drink and signaled for another. "No kidding. You must have seen hundreds of them in your practice."

"Which ones? Weddings or divorces?" He took out two whiskey glasses from under the bar and carried them to the kitchen.

I yelled after him, chewing on the olives: "Divorces. I mean, you must've seen more of them than weddings."

"Yes, isn't that strange?" he yelled back. "There are more people getting married than there are getting divorced and yet, here we are, knowing more divorced ones than married ones."

I thought about the "we" in what he said. I was in the same boat as my boss. I wasn't sure why that hadn't sunk in before. "It's not that strange. It's your business, after all."

"Yes. And business is always very good. Two lumps?"

"Yeah," I yelled. He knew I liked my old-fashioned sweet, but he always asked anyway. I heard the plop of sugar cubes and the sound of him muddling them with bitters in each glass. Each slosh and crunch reminded me of someone mixing cement. "So, what are your numbers?"

"One hundred and nineteen divorces, including the three pending. I've only been to one wedding."

"One wedding?"

"One."

"Whose?"

The muddling stopped and I heard my boss tap the mixing spoons on the brim of each respective glass before setting them down and returning to the bar. "Mine."

"Yours?" I asked, suddenly straightening my back. "You're divorced?"

"No, I had a wedding. Big difference." He free-poured two fingers of bourbon into each glass and began to stir each exactly fifty rotations, like I had seen him do many times before.

Feeling as if I was getting too familiar, I started to apologize, but he stopped me midway with the wave of his spoon. He reached down into the freezer under the bar and pulled out a large ice cube for each glass. With the ice in the drinks, he stirred them another fifty rotations.

"Sorry," my boss said. "It might make it easier for me to tell you about it if you told me about yours, first."

"Mine? I've never been married before."

"Girlfriends? Boyfriends? Sorry if it's too personal. Sexual harassment and everything."

"Hey, I'm wearing your clothes and drinking at your place. I think we're past that already." I laughed. "No, man. We're cool. We're friends. It's all right you ask."

"I'm sorry."

"No, don't be," I said and, before it got more awkward, added, "People think of me differently when they know I'm gay right off the bat."

"Why's that?"

"I don't know," I replied, unsure of myself and what I was trying to say, who I was supposed to be besides what other people thought of me. "Sometimes people think I want more than a conversation or a drink when they find out. Sometimes they find out and think I've been hiding a whole different person."

In the silence that followed, I looked up at the table and, under his stoic stare, I thought I saw a slight crack of hurt. "But you're cool," I floundered, "I don't think you're like that at all! Are you gay, too?"

"Thanks. I'm not gay. But I guess that's the difference: I don't feel like I have to say it, while you feel like you can't." He stopped stirring and went for an orange on the bar. He thumbed down two peels with a paring knife.

"I've only ever had two real relationships in my life," I said. "Whatever else isn't worth mentioning."

He pinched a zest of orange peel in each glass before proceeding to rub the waxy rind around their lips. "Any one of those two you thought about marrying?"

"Sure. But the more we talked about marriage, the more it scared us, you know? I mean, our parents would kill us. Even now."

"Your parents don't know you're gay?"

"Hell no. And with my brother dead, there's even more pressure for me to, you know, carry on the family name."

"I see. That sounds more difficult than some." My boss dropped the peels into the glasses and brought the drinks over to the table.

"Maybe. I don't know. Every relationship has its issues. Look at how many people are getting divorced."

He placed one of the old-fashioneds in front of me and took a seat. The rich copper sheen of the liquid cut through the glass and bled like a golden aura around our drinks. At the right angle, they looked like two suns between us. "Just because there are issues doesn't mean people get a divorce, but that's always the reason, isn't it? A problem leads to a separation. We could have all these problems, but it just takes the one."

"Some problems just eclipse the rest."

"Yeah." My boss grinned and took a sip of his drink. He looked at it before putting it down, as if trying to find the rest of his words inside. I took a taste in turn, the complexity of bitter, sweet, tart, and smoky hitting my nose and washing over my tongue. We sipped our drinks in silence until he huffed, put his glass aside, and continued.

"I wasn't always from around here. The first time I stepped into the States, I was sixteen going on seventeen. Back home, I was already married, but it wasn't anything official. I gave her a cat instead of a wedding ring. Cute, huh?"

I nodded and thought of a cat curled up in my glass.

"Her name was Pat-Pat. The cat, not the girl. Her name was Faith. Anyway, I went to college here and I told her to wait for me. The girl, not the cat. I'd study hard, get my citizenship, master the law, and petition to get her here. Three years went by and I did everything up to the point of petitioning for her. All the while, we emailed and called each other, our relationship growing deeper and deeper. I have known no deeper connection than the one I had with Faith.

"But as our love blossomed, Pat-Pat got older and older. She lost her sight first, then her appetite, and then, finally, hid under Faith's bed and died. We were really pushing for her to live. I sent money home to pay for the medical bills. Faith made sure she got her medicine and curled up with her every night. We both prayed the rosary every day. Despite all that, our cat still died. She was gone. And without her, our relationship was over. Once Faith told me, we both said our goodbyes. I haven't spoken to her since. That was five years ago."

While I digested my boss's story, I watched as the cat inside my glass uncurled itself. As it stepped out, I followed it to the edge of the table, where the animal dropped down into the lap of my boss's barong. I picked up my drink again and tried to enjoy it, but its taste had somehow been sullied.

"That can't be the only reason you two broke up. There had to be other things."

My boss brought his old-fashioned to his lips. He patted

the barong beside him as if it had been the one who told the story. "Sure, there were other things, but that was the main reason. Sorry if it sounds silly. Like I said, your reasons are worse than mine, probably."

"I mean, there's also the fact that she was taking care of that cat herself. I'm sure she had her own problems on top of that serious responsibility you put on her. Come on, man, a cat?"

"I know, she must have felt relieved Pat-Pat was gone, huh?" my boss said.

"Sorry, I don't mean to torture you, but there is definitely more to it, isn't there?"

"Maybe. Sometimes there's more. Sometimes it's just a cat."

Bewildered by the story my boss told me, I left that night feeling silly to be borrowing his barong. What had happened between my boss, Faith, and the cat seemed so ridiculous, and yet I could not stop comparing it to what continued to happen between my boss, myself, and his barong. Before, when I used to put on his barong, I'd feel more confident and empowered, as if somehow what made my boss who he was had been sewn into its stitching.

But after hearing his story, what I borrowed became just as transparent as the act. For years, I wanted to learn more about him and forget more about myself. For years, we had fallen into this type of relationship. This connection. Were we tied together by something so delicate? So absurd?

By the time I put it on for my cousin's wedding, my boss's

barong had lost all its power. The collar itched, the sleeves were tight, and everything underneath showed completely through the dull patterns. To make matters worse, when I arrived at the wedding, I was the only one wearing a barong, so I easily stood out among the crowd. In my discomfort, I felt exposed to all of my relatives and friends. The barong had become less an object of distinction and more like a target on my back. For every lola who would compliment the seams and how *guapo* I looked, there would be three Kuyas and a Tita who would call me *tamad* or lazy.

Everyone had something to say, and suddenly, I realized I had nothing to say for it myself. Suddenly, the barong became a burden. I had put on something I was no more a part of than my boss's cat was of his relationship.

That night, after the wedding, I thought of the cat, and my brother's hands returned in my dreams. Except now they were accompanied by fire, the hands even more vivid in their light than they had ever been. The skin of his tightly closed fists crackled and bubbled while the cones disintegrated and the paper waved with each whip of the flame.

The next day, I phoned my boss and immediately went to his house to tell him about it. To my surprise, he wasn't wearing his barong. He didn't even make me a drink.

"So, your dreams are worse now," he said, beckoning me inside.

"Yeah. Ever since you told me about the cat." I shut the door, still carrying his barong by the hanger. It hovered beside me like a wraith.

"I told you. Sometimes cats do that." He stood at the table, folding something on a plate.

I came closer and noticed the bananas and egg wrappers on the table. "You're making *turon*?" I said, and hung the barong on a chair.

"Yeah, they're my favorite. You ever make them before?"

"No, only watched."

"You want to try? It's not hard. I did most of the prep work already." He placed a bowl of halved bananas coated in brown sugar between us. "You need to wash your hands. I'll get you a bowl of water. It's the binder for the wrapper. Gotta wet the edges."

Before I could refuse, I washed my hands and carried my bowl of water and plate back to the table. As if under a spell, I had fallen into my boss's pace again.

"Put an egg wrapper flat on your plate, then put one of the saba banana slices horizontally at the bottom of it."

I pinched the long slice of banana and did as instructed. "Shouldn't there be jackfruit in this?"

"I don't do mine with that. Sorry. Just the saba banana."

"Saba? I always thought it was just regular banana in here."

"You can use any banana. But the Filipino saba banana is best warmed up in this."

I compared what I remembered—glistening shells hiding

molten centers of sweet mush—with what we were making—cold, dull, and inert exigence in a delicate sheath. As we folded the wrappers around our bananas and rolled them into *turon*, I wondered if this was really what they had always been. Bananas look like bananas until they're not.

After we finished wrapping the *turon*, we brought them to the kitchen where the oil was already heated in a pot. My boss proceeded to pick out each prepared piece one by one and slowly lowered them in. The *turon* crackled and wheezed as they turned golden brown in mere seconds. My boss talked over their molten roars: "They're transparent in the beginning, but you know they're done when you can't see what's inside at all."

When they were done, he plated the *turon* over a paper towel and let them rest before us, the sweet aroma of caramelized banana stewing in crispy egg wrapper and wafting in a pleasant heat.

"I've burned myself many times making this," he said. "There's no avoiding it. The oil's always going to jump out of the pot. And if the cooking doesn't get me, sometimes I'll burn my tongue eating it too soon. Just a burst of oil or scalding banana! Pop!"

In the *turon*, I saw my brother and his family, my boss and Faith, my relationships and who I was to others and myself, all the what-ifs I had had up to that point, the cat. They were all there before me, too hot to touch, transformed.

"Sometimes I wish it was me. Not him."

"Your brother?"

I nodded.

"You can't think that. The fact is, it wasn't you. It never will be you."

"Did Faith move on after the cat?"

"She did. Had another cat without me. Divorced, go figure, but happy. You don't need anyone else to have a cat."

"How can you do it?" I asked. "How can you live with all the divorce, man? Doesn't it make you feel depressed seeing these people want nothing more than to be apart?"

"On the contrary," my boss said, reaching out for one of the *turon* way before it was ready. I could see how hot it was even from the outside as a profuse amount of steam emanated from its surface, and it was even more clear when I saw its insides. What was there had not melted away. What was there stayed and merely became something new. "People separating are always thinking about how it was when they were together. For better or worse."

In the mall, my brother held the two melting ice cream cones, but he couldn't feel them. By then, the fire was all around them, and what was happening before him felt like it was happening to someone else, a long time ago. Whatever distance separated them, in a matter of moments, it didn't matter.

Promise Me More

The night the house collapsed, Noni and her mother, Delia Deleon Veracruse, were having a superfluous debate over what the lapels were called on her white suit—an homage to Sandy Powell's brilliant and heroic calico number at the BAFTA Awards. They had finished their dinner of tilapia, garlic fried rice, and coffee—no soda because, oh, they were on a diet—when Delia rose from her seat, startling Noni with the crash of the tower of old VHS tapes by the leg of her chair and the flap of old magazines by the leg of the table. Noni bent down to pick up what she could, inadvertently tipping over another pile, this time a stack of newspapers from the early 2000s. She pored over pictures of George Bush and people covered in ash running in the street while Delia ranted down at her. She could feel her mother's spittle and fury like the virgin pinpricks of a storm. She could see the cuff of her coat darken in dust.

"*Sulapa*. They are called *sulapa*," Delia insisted.

"It's *lapel* in English, Mom. You're not wrong. You're just using the wrong language. You're getting it confused with Tagalog," Noni said, still looking down at the papers. She folded a withered review of the first *Pirates of the Caribbean* movie from her four-hundred-dollar Air Jordans.

"Noni, you're the confused one. I haven't spoken that island jive in forty years."

"Jesus, Mom," Noni hooted. "Island jive?"

"It's not racist if I'm Filipino. I'm more Filipino than you. Remember that."

"I didn't call you racist. What's that thing around your shoulders called?"

"A Manila shawl," Delia said, closing it more tightly around her nape.

"See, Mom? It's just called a shawl! You've definitely got more Filipino in you."

"No, it's just I have more fashioned sense. Don't insult me."

Noni let Delia's continued misspeaking go without further correction. "I'm not insulting you. You're just Filipino, Mom."

She looked up at her mother's face. It was a mix of horror, disgust, and shame foreign to the present moment. The house groaned in the silence like an empty stomach. Standing before her, Delia was moving further and further back, regressing to the age of perms and her pristine house with the tacky orange carpet, now a crypt for mountains of devalued remembrances and cold wooden floors. Noni wondered who in her memory had taught her mom to call her language "island jive" and the importance of not sounding like you came from anywhere in a country where everyone was from everywhere.

Noni visited Delia and her childhood home every chance she got, although the frequency had dwindled the closer she got to her girlfriend, Rupee. Rupee was a gem she had discovered at the gallery she curated. Another first-generation Filipina traversing the art world with an arsenal of art degrees, fashion sense, Diaspora, and pithy art criticism to help them sell canvases for five figures. Her medium was acrylic imposed on old clippings. Think Poons meets Afremov meets a magazine rack. Noni's medium was whatever sold. Think someone who wasn't an artist but who could appreciate it enough to find value in it. Of course they fell in love. What was art without its lights and darks? What was love without its contrasts?

They dated for months before finally sleeping together—an ordeal, as Rupee had only slept with men and Noni had never slept with anyone—but they managed to figure things out. Despite her inexperience with the physical, Noni always had an acute understanding of the emotional side of relationships. It was an ability tempered by her profusely emotive mother, Delia Deleon Veracruse. She was a firebrand of dancing, screaming pain and pleasure, happiness and sadness. Delia's house had been full of her voice, her touch, her soul. Noni had to live with the weight of it so as not to be crushed, to have a spark of her own. Her mother was a storm she had to weather. She knew how to live with mood swings. She knew how to tame and live with a wild heart.

When her husband passed away, a decade before the house collapsed, Delia spent an entire year nude and confined to her home. She called it her newest performance art piece, "the unraveling of her portrait," but only Noni understood it for what it was: grieving. In her early years, Delia had been an art professor and proponent of civil rights at an all-white college that labeled her originality as "exotic," and defined her intelligence based on how well she spoke without an accent and how many remedies she could share for lightening your skin. Five years after retiring, Delia was naked and in her sixties, and Noni could see the toll that her mother's career had taken. Her arms, neck, and face were lighter than the skin she had been hiding underneath. The darkest part, her sex, was peppered gray and white. Her true self showed. Noni imagined that only she and her father knew what this looked like.

Like a trapeze artist balancing on a rope, Noni made her way through the clutter that filled the house, stepping thoughtfully so as not to knock over a stack of outdated encyclopedias here, a jade Buddha missing two fingers there. After her year in the nude, her mother put her clothes back on and spent the next couple of years unboxing things from the garage and storage. She was looking for an old photo album one day, a dress with butterfly sleeves the next, an old *parol* to put up for Christmas, and so on. The piles grew. Noni was amazed how much her mother had kept, but she should have known. She should have known they had a problem.

An hour before the house collapsed, she and her mother traversed through a home filled with physical manifestations of her compulsions. They found their way to the living room and found seats, an overturned trash bin cushioned with a satin pillow and a wooden chair, an *abularyo* blessed with calamansi and sampaguita petals. Above them, Delia had replaced her crystal chandelier with an old bar fixture that read *Red Horse Lager*. Light poked out of holes in the paint and made arbitrary lines across the ceiling. Coupled with the dim brown glow emanating from its warped plastic and falling on everything like a tawdry veil, this made the thing look like a dying star.

"As I was saying, about this suit," Noni began, picking a cobweb off her shoulder, "this famous costume designer wore a suit like this one to an award ceremony and got a ton of celebrities to sign their names on it for a charity of hers." She had quelled Delia's anger earlier by taking a fabric pen from her breast pocket and writing her name on her sleeve. This took her mother off guard long enough to move them to the living room and closer to the door. Noni had not thought of leaving yet, but being close to the exit made the passage safer for her suit, which was nearly impossible for her to keep clean in Delia's house.

Delia inched forward on her wastebasket and looked at the signature Noni left on her wrist. "Wow. How much did it sell for?"

"I don't know if she sold it yet, but it had Robert De Niro, Al Pacino, Joaquin Phoenix, Scarlett Johansson, Laura Dern, Brad Pitt—"

"Who's Walking Phoenix?"

"Joaquin."

"That's what I said. Who is he?"

"The one who played that depressed clown."

"Oh yes, sad. Wow," Delia said in awe. "But why did you write on your suit?"

"It's meant to be written on, Mom. It's art." Noni took out her fabric pen again. She stuck the cap on its bottom and held it out to her mother. "You give it a try. Write something, whatever you want."

"Oh no, Noni. I can't. It's so white. I'll ruin it," Delia said, her hands gathered under her chin, gripping her shawl, eyes still on the tip of the pen.

Noni waved it like a conductor. "You won't ruin it. If anything, you'll just be adding value to it."

"I don't think my name's worth anything, Noni. I'm no Walking Phoenix."

"Joaquin."

"Yes, I'm no Scarlett Johansson."

The house bellowed again, this time with a slight shake. In the first couple of years, Noni came over to help her mother every Sunday. She was in her late twenties, and things in the gallery were slow but lucrative enough. She pored over each article they uncovered like an artifact. There was a story with a coffee machine, an old comforter, a bin of hats. Some of these memories Noni shared with Delia. The baggie of dead batteries labeled "Noni's nightlight," her Barbie backpack she'd worn on her first day of school. Others, only Delia Deleon Veracruse kept stowed away in the spirit of laughter and tears. There was the rusted machete with a leather sheath and broken handle, the carving of a goat missing its face, the shoebox of candy wrappers flattened by an iron and bound in string. Everything had value, even if its value was unknown.

"Come on, Mom, it doesn't matter. I want you to write your name on me," Noni said, following her mother back to the kitchen. She winced as the heel of her shoe was scratched by a metal fan with a dragon pattern. She nearly cried when the hem of her pants caught and tore on a plastic bonsai tree.

"Don't ruin good clothes, Noni," Delia said, and ran water into the empty tin container from the rice maker.

"You're not ruining it! If you think so, how about writing your name under my *sulapa*?"

"Don't patronize me," she puffed from the sink as she scraped the dregs of burned rice off with her fingernails.

"I'm not trying to patronize you! I really want to you to write on me, Mom. Really, I wore this suit for you," Noni half-lied. She had worn it as part of her gallery's "dismantling project." The goal: to get Filipinos to sign it and put it up for sale. The aim: to put it up during a show without a price so that, if someone asked, she could explain that it was not for sale, that no exorbitant financial value or act of contrition can be exchanged for a life, that wanting the suit wasn't as important as having your name on it. That or some other bullshit to get enough publicity and clout for the actual pieces with price tags. She knew it would be easier if she explained this to her mother, but she also knew Delia liked not being told. She liked the mystery, the drama.

Still, Noni wanted so badly to explain to her mother that where Powell's suit was trying desperately to save her teacher's home—a notable hub for underrepresented artists and intellectuals—her enclave's white suit was trying to dismantle a metaphorical one—the auction house of the oppressor in which the value of one's identity is weighed. She wondered if Delia would appreciate this irony. Alas, messages were lost if they were explained, Delia had taught Noni.

And things don't sell themselves, Noni had taught herself.

Delia lifted her hands from the container and rinsed them under the faucet. "I won't write my name."

"Fine. Then how about you draw something?"

Delia stepped over a dusty bread box and dried her hands

on the kitchen towel hanging on the oven door. "Jesus, I don't know how that's any better."

"Look, like this." Noni drew a butterfly under her signature. She held it up over a stack of calendars from Seafood City. The one on the top read 2012–2014 and had the picture of a smiling husky on the cover. "See? It's nice. Not tacky at all."

"*Mura* is more like it."

"What? Is that one of your English-not-Tagalog words again?"

"It means cheap. *Mura, mura.*"

Noni rose her wrist to her eyes. "Ok, it's not the best butterfly."

"Besides, butterflies are not anything special. They are attracted to rotten, dirty things just like any other fly. They smell the salt in our sweat and blood and waste. They crave it."

"They want to eat us?"

"Yes, but their mouths are too small for you to feel them trying to suck the life out of you. People forgive them because they are beautiful, but they are ravenous and filthy. I don't like them."

"They fly on shit?"

"Yes. A lot of shit. Don't use that word."

"Shit. Remind me not to let one of those things land on me again."

The windows creaked and the walls crackled. Above, the weight of exercise machines, baby clothes, Christmas lights, musical instruments, geodes, fossils, car parts, bicycles, autographed portraits, masterful forgeries, originals, Noni's diaries, and everything else kept and unseen on the second floor leaned on rotten, brittle beams ready to give way. Everything was succumbing to years of accumulation. Nothing would be saved.

By the sixth year of the hoarding, Noni finally recognized her mother's actions as a problem and approached her about the topic. At first, she did it in a subtle way. She suggested her mother watch Marie Kondo's special on Netflix and forwarded several links on tidying up her home, hoping she would come to her own realization about the state of her living conditions. However, as Delia continued to crowd her house, Noni decided to try more direct approaches at the risk of upsetting her.

First, she tried talking to her directly. Mom, she would start, and then an interrogation of her actions: *What are you looking for? Why are you doing this? When does this end?*

But, of course, Delia escaped these words like a fly escaping clapped hands.

I'm looking for A. Because of B. This ends when I find C.

The answers always stopped Noni from digging deeper and, in her frustration, she would carry on, sorting through old copies of the same Carpenters record for the one with the Circuit City label on it, clinking through empty glass candle holders trying to find the one with Jesus holding a lamb, Saint Lorenzo Ruiz hanging upside down, his hands in prayer as samurai watched from their horses, katanas drawn.

Then, finally, without any options left, Noni began taking things from the house. In the beginning, she would take things that her mother wouldn't miss: a few clothes here, a couple of old unused stamps there. Then she began taking bigger things: a bust of Athena, a dozen rolls of rugs. She would stuff them into her car and drive to the closest dumpster before her mother would notice. But Delia filled the house faster than Noni could take things away. Paintings were replaced with posters, tubs of chalk exchanged for tubs of molding clay. If Delia noticed, she never mentioned it. The house filled more and more as Noni came and took less and less.

Now, fifteen minutes before the collapse, Noni decided to take something from Delia right in front of her eyes. She would casually grab it, announce her removal of it, and leave with it no matter what happened. She was determined to get a response that elicited some change. All that needed to be decided was what.

"If you're not going to write on my suit then I will have to take . . ." she commenced, but couldn't decide on anything. Her eyes went from the magazines at her feet to the clocks marring the kitchen counter.

"What will you take?" Delia said, her voice unmoved from its default charm, her tailored American accent.

Noni continued to look around. There was too much to

choose from, and the longer she took to decide, the more she hesitated. "I will take other measures."

"Such as?" her mother asked.

Above the sink were empty flower vases sitting on the windowsill. By the drying rack, an array of mugs. There was her father's green mug with the chip on the handle, her mother's yellow *The Little Prince* mug, Noni's old robin mug that had graduated from brushes to hidden dime bags of weed to coffee. Branches outside of the window rasped the glass. The mugs rattled more than they should have.

"Such as . . ." Noni repeated, moving now, hopping over a pile of *Seventeen* magazines, darting past the three-foot-tall, four-foot-wide bronze statue of stampeding horses. She squatted before the garbage bags of Beanie Babies, parted a rack of plastic-clad coats. All the while, her mother watched her, following where her hands went in anticipation. Their hearts pounded in their chests so hard they did not notice the whine and sag of the ceiling, the stucco molting like snowflakes. Neither did they notice the white suit continue to collect wounds of refuse and debris, ashes at the arms, the shoulders, the seams, the knees.

Noni saw the wildness in Delia's eyes begin to surface.

Delia saw her daughter roaming through her most precious things like a child carelessly running her hands through tall grass, at any moment ready to pluck a blade.

Frog

"Did you say *Chrono Trigger*?" Lina asks, her lips slightly agape, exposing a dark green tongue. I stare a little too long at her mouth, discolored by the dye the bar used for her "Marlboro Breath" cocktail, still trying to place her voice.

She was one of Luke's friends, the one he was telling me would be here if I would only come with him (Please? Just once?) to the "super-rad" video game bar down the street from our office.

"They got good booze, and she's a voice actress. Didn't you want to be one of those in high school?" he commented, and before I could deny it, we were here.

Lina's voice was familiar in the way that I recognized it only when it was addressing other people. In other conversations, she transformed from one familiar character to another, from a creature who could communicate only by repeating her own name to a young boy who piloted a giant robot.

Somehow, her talking directly to me, shoulder to shoulder, made her sound like no one.

The game we had been playing at our table was simple. We each took turns asking the group for one video game that had the kind of character we described. The person whose turn it was would say, "Name a game where a character uses a big sword," and someone would reply *Final Fantasy 7*, another, *Soulcalibur V*. There wasn't a penalty for not replying, there wasn't one for getting it wrong or saying the same thing as someone else, other than a less sober person than you spurring you on to pick another. There was no winning or losing the game, either. It was a game just to stir the pot, just to get conversation going. It ended when someone had to go, when someone started the domino of leaving, one "I have to get up early" after another "I got a long drive."

Luke puffed the last request, "Name a game where a frog's a hero."

"*Frogger*," someone spat.

"*Battle Toads*. Does that count?" another replied.

"*Chrono Trigger*," I said.

"Did you say *Chrono Trigger*?" Lina asked, more like a whisper after my thinking about it, after my staring at her emerald lips for an embarrassingly long time.

I can't tell if it is my words or her repeating them that give them the final nudge, but it dislodges the memories of my grandmother, my lola, I hadn't thought about in years. I turn

from Lina and see flashes of them reflected in the bitter am-
ber of my "Cosmo Canyon"—an old-fashioned absolutely
nothing like the one Tifa shook for Cloud. The clap of her *ts-
inelas* on her plastic floor runners, the whiff of her garlic rice
and fried fish breakfast wafting from each blow to the game
cartridge when it didn't work, then the padded smack of her
pushing it into the slot of the console and sliding up the power switch, a purple button that flicked up instead of sank in.

"Sa-*Star Fox*!" someone stutters.

"PaRappatherapper!" another says overeagerly.

"Does that count?" the one who said *Battle Toads* asks.

Luke nods. "The Rastafarian Frog's a little racist, but I'll
allow it."

"Did you say *Chrono Trigger*?" Lina asks again, except this
time I know it's a whisper, I know they are words meant just
for me, but I still try to ignore them. I look at the TVs stream-
ing games of *Smite* and *League of Legends*, the "Foxdie" and
"Blue Shell" and "Nukashine" and all the other overpriced,
elaborately named cocktails the bar has to offer. I try anything to avoid looking at her mouth again and suddenly, I
hear someone else, I see someone else's lips part and thin. My
lola's shouts beckon me to her where she stews, between the
blue fuzz of static and the awkward shadows steam makes in
the light.

"Did you die again?" she asks from the *plantsa*, an iron in
hand, hissing, "*Aye, tanga!* Did you save the game?"

On the floor before the television, I feel the SNES controller nearly slip out of my sweaty hands. My head turns from the swinging pendulum of the opening screen, the 8-bit tics of time ushering the rising scale, my lola's angry face coming into view like the crescent half of the clock unveiling the title, the words yet to follow.

When my lola got this upset, I knew she loved the game as much as I did. Video games were how she learned English when she immigrated from the Philippines to the States, how we learned to communicate and bond. She was always buying me new games, always urging me to play, always watching. Her joy was my joy, my game was her game.

But before I can tell her yes or no, someone yawns, "Whelp, I got work in the morning," and the dominos fall, one after another, slowly pulling me from the bar and out of Lola's house.

Outside, Luke is too hammered to drive so someone calls him a Lyft. I tell everyone I'll wait with him, and to have a good night. The ones that know each other say their goodbyes, the ones that don't know anyone leave before everyone else. Lina is gone before I know which she is: the voluptuous mage from the anime or the loli demon from the JRPG. It is only a little past eight, but everyone like us, who go to bars early and only order one drink, have places they would rather be. I only knew Luke, but how Luke knew these people, I didn't know. Before I can ask, Luke's Lyft comes and I'm already putting him in the back, buckling him into his seat.

"I can do that. I'm not a baby," he slurs, but despite his opposition, he raises his arms and doesn't get in my way.

"I'll see you next week," I say.

"Next week? Oh yeah, tomorrow's Friday, we don't work tomorrow."

"You don't work. I do."

"Oh yeah. Where does time go? Wasn't that fun? Parrapa the Rarara. Parrapa the Rararar . . ." he says, failing to finish before I shut the door and the car drives away.

Where does time go? In the time it takes to get from the corner to my car, I think of several answers. In *The Ocarina of Time*, you can go to the future, but you change from a child to an adult. You literally waste seven years of your life. You're the same ocarina-tooting, pot-smashing, grass-whacking forest boy who ran away from home that you were seven years ago, except you're an adult now with the Master Sword and the things you did in the past didn't really amount to what you expected them to. Time's moved on without you, and you're stuck in the future trying to start all over again.

My lola hands me *Chrono Trigger* for the first time. I am the same then as I am now, I think, except much shorter. On the cover, Crono, the silent protagonist with the spiky red hair, is lunging up at a monster while Marle, a runaway princess, is casting fire to his sword. On the ground, at the tip of my thumbs, is who I think is just another monster hunched over in the snow until I play the game and realize it's another ally, Frog, helping Crono leap off his back.

"Lola! Look at this frog!" I point to the screen.

She pulls a thread from her repurposed cookie tin and looks up from repairing a fresh hole in my pants. I was always ripping them, she was always sewing them.

As Frog ribbits and does his signature flex after winning a battle, she cackles, exposing her checkered teeth as if there's another game in her mouth. "*Nakakatawang lalaking palaka!* He's a cute! Make sure you level him up, *anakong*!" However, before long, he's gone from my party, and I'm worried I'll never see him again.

But in *Chrono Trigger*, no one is gone forever. You keep traveling, back and forth, through time. Eventually, everything you do and everyone you meet comes back to you.

"*Chrono Trigger.*"

The words cut through the night like Frog using his mythical sword, Masamune, to cut through a cliff, exposing a path to the next dungeon.

"Everyone's gone," they say, and I think it's the one-eyed sell-sword from the mercenary guild before I turn to find Lina following me.

I'm so surprised, I just nod.

"That's the best Link impression I ever seen. Or should I say Crono?" she says.

"Who?" I reply and immediately regret it. I know I should've

laughed, I know I should've been excited that she was refer-
encing two characters from some of my favorite games ever.
Instead, my barrier is up, the one I cast when I want to refrain
from acknowledging I ever enjoyed things to appear more
professional or mature, like how Dan from *Street Fighter Al-
pha* refrains from acknowledging he doesn't know how to
fight even though he can't throw a real fireball to save his life.
I act like some arrogant asshole who knows less than he does,
and for what? The match is set, the timer flashes to KO, but
who really cares if it runs out or not but me?

I hear the rattle of tapping buttons echo from the distant
past. In the power lines above us, the sound of Crono's Single Tech, Cyclone, repeats itself, his sword slashes filling up
the screen, the monsters disappearing in a wash of red at the
empty intersection.

"*Chrono Trigger*," she repeats again, like another chance,
like another coin in the slot. She crosses her arms and leans
on the door of my Corolla.

"Oh, yeah, Link from *Zelda* and Crono from *Chrono Trigger*.
They don't talk. Good one." I say but it's too late to sound like
anything but insincere.

"It's been so long since I thought of that game!" she says,
and in the dark I cannot tell if her mouth is still green, if she's
smiling or frowning.

"I thought you left," I say, and afraid I am coming off rude again, I follow it up by asking why she's still around in a futile effort to recover.

"I actually left and came back. I left something at the bar. Carrre to help me look for it?" she says, and she rolls the "r" at the end of "care" like she's some cat or somebody pretending to be from a cartoon. I know it's a good impression, but my barrier is still up so I don't acknowledge it.

"Sure, I got nothing better to do. What did you lose?"

She pushes her back off my car and starts past me. "I lost my necklace. It just fell off, I guess. It does that," she says and, behind me, her voice sounds just like how Marle's did in my head all those years ago. Leene's Bell rings as Crono and her bump into each other for the first time. The music stops and my barrier fades. All the exits are blocked and the bell continues to ring until you've retrieved what she's lost.

"Like Marle at the Millennial Fair?" I say, hearing my lola try to direct me to the object pulsing white on the screen. "Over there! *Doon!*" she screams over my shoulder.

"Like who?" Lina asks.

I turn to Lola but she's zoned into the game, pointing with her lips at the screen. "You know, from—"

"I'm just playing with you! Yeah, it's exactly like that. You know that those who hear the bell ring are blessed with happy and fortunate lives?"

"What? They are?"

"That's what that little girl NPC says somewhere at the fair. I mean, it's kinda true."

"Yeah," I say and bring the necklace back to Marle. She asks if she can have it back and there are two options, yes or no. My lola doesn't say anything, but I can feel her waiting for me to make the right choice. "But," I continue, "you know, with the way the game plays out and how they originally meant for Crono to die in the Ocean Palace, maybe she was just full of shit."

"What?" she asks, and I think I've made a mistake, but Marle's already asked if she could tag along and I've already said yes. She introduces herself and the game asks me to input her name, but my lola tells me to keep what's there. "*Ito ang pangalan niya.* Why call her something else?"

"Oh, I just meant she was wrong." I say, my lola silent now, but never too far away.

Lina leans into me with the sharp nudge of her shoulder. "Fuck yeah, she's full of shit! Don't get me started on what they did in *Chrono Cross*. I was mortified! It really doesn't bode well for them no matter which of the thirteen endings you choose."

"Wasn't there twelve?"

"Technically," she says, the two of us approaching the bar again, ready for another round, "but 'Game Over' counts as an ending too."

Far from Home

Before all the video arcades closed thanks to the innovation of online gaming, Dad and I kept one in a little corner space between the rest of a mall and a Montgomery Ward (which was gone before we were, although the space they left was still empty). Besides the usual mall favorites like the shoe stores, fashion depots, and pretzel shops, the place was full of Filipino places catering to the large community of us in an area far from home. There were Filipino bakeries and fast-food restaurants, a barong shop, a karaoke stall, and a seafood market. Dad knew all the owners and patrons of these establishments. He was particularly friendly with the owner of the seafood market, Marie, who in turn was real sweet on me but never paid more attention to poor Dad than anyone else. Nevertheless, he was a popular and kind guy. Would rather toss some free tokens at kids than yell at them for breaking a machine. We had a small apartment by the mall, so we were never far from it. After school, I'd head to the arcade first. That was my real home. I never got into games like Dad did, but I liked getting my hands in the machines, figuring out how they worked. We had a decent life in that arcade. I couldn't say I wasn't happy.

When the arcade went under, Dad went with it, as if giving up the place also meant giving up who he was. He stopped working, stopped talking, stopped going out, stopped caring for himself. His friends kept calling, but he never picked up. He would just sit on the balcony and look down, waiting. Says a lot about me for not talking to him about it, or at least chaining up that sliding door to the balcony. But what could I do? Dad wasn't the only one hurting. While he sat there, I got older, stayed out later, and eventually found my own job at the mall working at the seafood market for Marie. It wasn't like looking into Dad's old machines, but it was work.

Dad disappeared on my eighteenth birthday. All his things were still in their place. His room still smelled like he was there. The police and his friends couldn't do anything but tweet about it. Nobody looked for him. When I told Marie, she put me on full-time with benefits even though my hours were far from it.

"You need to think about yourself right now." She coughed and put her hand on my shoulder.

She was always sick on account of how cold we had to keep the market for the fish. She constantly smelled like fish guts and Vicks VapoRub.

"Your dad had it rough. That doesn't mean you should have it that way too."

I graduated from high school and started working the full forty a week. Still, Dad didn't return. Why would he? I thought. Sometimes a problem just goes away.

◆ ◆ ◆

Three years after Dad disappeared, I received your letter addressed to him. It was postmarked from Mindanao to the mall's address, one year before our arcade closed. Marie handed it to me while I was labeling some jars and told me to take a break.

"Take your time with that," she sniffled, standing over me, the strong menthol odor of the VapoRub and the sour smell of fish blood trailing after her like a ghost. "The jars will be waiting for you when you return."

By then I knew more than jars. I could name and identify all the fish we had at the market. There were your *alumahan*, *bisugo*, and *kitang*; the popular ones like your salmon, tilapia, *bangus*, *galunggong*, *maya-maya*, and *dilis*; and your more exotic fare that only the older folks bought like your *sapsap*, *hiwas*, and *lapu-lapu*. There was something more fulfilling in knowing fish than in knowing the inside of a machine.

I took the letter to the break room and opened it on the table over some crumbs and a wet spot from someone's lunch.

At the top of the letter was Dad's name preceded by the word "dear" printed in lowercase. Based on your handwriting, you were unfamiliar with what you were writing but tried to express all you could with all you knew.

Return. Recome. Relate. Respond. Goodbye.

The words were followed by strange markings. At first, I thought they might have been drawings. The shapes took the form of animals I had never seen before, but among them was a particular pattern and intent beyond the arbitrary. Toward the end, whatever was already on the table bled through and smeared the ink. I quickly lifted the paper, but the damage was done. Something I already couldn't understand became even more indecipherable. I spent hours in the break room trying to figure it out. Eventually, it was closing time, and Marie and I were the last ones left in the mall.

"This is an invitation and a ticket home," she rasped, clearing her throat. She proceeded to tell me that she and Dad came from the same island tucked in the rough waters of the Sulu Sea. It was far removed from the rest of the Philippines, from modernization, and from the Islamic influences in the south. Dad never spoke of it.

Marie had kept where she was from a secret, but somehow, Dad knew. From what Marie told me, there was a connection everyone on the island had with it and each other. Home was an island where there was no technology, just two indigenous tribes still living by the old ways and worshipping the old ones. I tried to imagine the island but all I could see was the arcade beyond the fish on their bed of ice. I couldn't imagine a place without technology or even a place where fish were alive.

As for the old ways and the old ones, my father had raised me Catholic my entire life. In his room was a tiny altar nailed to his wall, a porcelain Santo Niño standing at its center. I slept with a rosary and a relic of Saint Peregrine in my pocket. But, according to Marie, the old ones were our gods. Although she and my father had learned to be devout Catholics, religion had nothing to do with the old ones. The old ones existed no matter what one believed. Some called them the *Datus* or the *Taong-lupa*, but they really had neither name nor form. Those things did not matter to them. They kept the island and its tribes safe. And, in return, the people abided by their rules.

Marie told me the story of the island's tribes and about the consequence for leaving. Before the old ones, the two tribes, the Dumama and Jokoko, were constantly at war over fish and pearls until each commodity became scarce. The old ones, in the form of a storm, promised to provide fish and protection to both tribes if they stopped fighting and accepted their law. The tribes agreed and lived in harmony and prosperity with the old ones.

"Since then," said Marie, "our people have kept to the island

and to the same way of life they had been used to for thousands of years."

Among these traditions were two very important ones: no one could leave the island, and the Dumama and Jokoko had to intermarry to have children. The tribes were content with this until, a thousand years later, a few people wanted to leave. The old ones did not force people to stay, but there was a price for safe passage to the outside world: the person who left would have to leave behind the person they loved most and never return again.

I assumed this was how Marie ended up in the States and why she did not want to talk about it, so I didn't pursue her reasons further. Instead, I thought about Dad and about me. When I came to the States, I was too young to remember anything before that. As far as I knew, I had always been here and never anywhere else. I had nothing else.

Marie told me that the language I could not recognize was the writing of the Dumama, the tribe she belonged to.

"I've had to change so much from back then in order to blend in with the people here," she murmured from deep in her throat. I could not imagine how her people dressed or how much she really had to change. I could not imagine Marie any other way. She was always trying to fight something off, always working hard to live. It was hard to imagine her not struggling.

Marie read the letter and told me that you were inviting me

back. She speculated that because I had not chosen to leave the island, I could return now if I wanted to.

"You can go for a visit and see if you like it," Marie said, as if I could just snap my fingers and get there. I told her I didn't have any time or money to go anywhere, nor did I want to visit a place so far removed from what I already knew. The seafood market started to feel humid. Somewhere far off in the mall, I thought I heard the crash of waves.

"It's too late," Marie said. She held out the letter and pointed where the table had stained the writing, but her voice and face were already far away. "Once this gets wet and dries, you're already there."

I was hit with a wall of salt water and seaweed on a long expanse of sand. I was no longer sitting on a chair with a table and Marie in front of me. Instead, I was sitting in a shallow tide, waves dancing beyond the horizon at sunset. I closed my eyes, and when I opened them again my legs were sinking in the sand, my uniform drenched below my waist. I was there on your island.

◆ ◆ ◆

People of all ages dressed in orange and purple garments trudged through the heavy sand to meet me. I began to make out their village extending over the water, its appearance becoming more apparent in the dimming light. I got up and walked toward them, surprisingly unafraid. In some strange way, these people felt familiar to me.

At the front of the line was an old man with a vibrant head-dress of banana leaves fanning out above his ears. Other than a mild slouch, his stride was swift despite his age. In fact, he moved as fast as even the strongest-looking of them. He walked toward me, an inviting smile on his face, his arms raised to show he meant no harm. They all looked friendly. Reflexively, I raised my arms too.

I was surprised that I understood their language. Maybe Dad had spoken it while I slept, and it had soaked into my subconscious. They all welcomed me, repeating the words "*Tabi-Tabi po*," the men slapping my back, the women wrangling their children, who were watching curiously from behind their mothers' skirts. I saw myself in the eyes of one little boy, behind whose wonder lurked a curled yet pensive fear of the unknown.

As we walked to the village, the old man introduced himself as the chief of the Jokoko. His people had been anticipating my visit. I asked him if he had seen Dad, but neither he nor anyone in the village had seen him since he left.

"The old ones," the chief of the Jokoko started, letting a little girl ride on his tan and toned shoulders, her feet beating at his chest, "only want to give people what they want."

The little girl on the chief's shoulders continued to repeat the words that greeted me on the beach. I asked the chief what "*Tabi-Tabi po*" meant, and he laughed, saying there had been a misunderstanding.

"At first, we thought you were one of them. '*Tabi-Tabi po*' is what you're supposed to say when you come across one of the old ones. You ask them to let you pass."

I asked the chief if he'd ever met a god, and the chief shook his head. He said that if he were to really meet a god, words would be unnecessary.

◆ ◆ ◆

The village was made up of densely clustered huts strewn across the shoreline and over the sea. The huts over the water, each occupied by an entire multigenerational household, were connected by plank and bamboo stilts. The reflection of the setting sun on the ocean's surface made it nearly opaque, but underneath I could see teeming shadows of life. The waves thrashed and rippled, but despite this frenzied activity, there were no fishing boats on the water.

All the work was done on land. Trays of *dilis* and *hiwas* lay salted and drying in the sun. Skewered *lapu-lapu* and blue crab hung over an open fire while rice steamed in banana leaves elevated far above clay furnaces. Young men and women cut freshly gathered herbs and vegetables, the smell of mint, cilantro, calamansi, ginger, and an assortment of colorful chili peppers distributing a pungent smell across the harbor.

As we traversed farther into the village, I grew curious about the Dumama and asked the chief where their village was. The chief touched his heart and said they were all around us, and I assumed he meant there was no distinguishing the tribes from one another. I told him about how I met a member of the Dumama and a glint of surprise showed on the chief's face before he covered it up with a smile.

"They only come out at night," he said and didn't speak again until we'd made it to his hut, the one farthest out in the ocean.

◆ ◆ ◆

Nearly a hundred people filled the chief's hut, bringing enough food to feed three times as many. The chief and I sat on cushioned seats at the main table while his people served us. From what I could recognize, there were the dried *dilis* and *hiwas*, grilled blue crab and *lapu-lapu*, and fresh, creamy sea urchin. I gorged on the smoky, salty taste of the freshly cooked fish. It was the first time I had really enjoyed eating it rather than looking at it. Had that been all the food I ate, I might've already been satisfied, but then a steaming pot of stew puffing with the aroma of chili peppers, coconut, and fatty fish made it to our table. The chief told me it was a nameless delicacy made to honor the old ones. The savory, sweet, and spicy sauce blended perfectly with the milky *bangus* and salmon-like fish melting in my mouth. With the salt of the ocean breeze brushing my lips and stinging my sweat-drenched skin, the stew seemed to envelope me more and more, bowl after bowl. By the end of the night, the pot was empty and the hall was cleared.

Still, the Dumama had not come. Food was put aside for them and brought to another hut for later. According to the chief, their absence was no surprise; the Dumama were very shy, especially with visitors. Hiding my disappointment, I apologized for inconveniencing them and helped him put together my makeshift bed of mats and wools. I told the chief that, although I appreciated his hospitality, I had already decided to leave in the morning. In the dark, I could not see him, but the unwavering kindness in his voice assured me that the Jokoko would respect my decision.

We settled in, but sleep did not come. My mind fixated on the sound of the water hitting the bamboo and thundering up and down the coast and far beyond the island. There was so much I did not know, and I was too curious about it to sleep. I quietly made my way out to explore. Outside the chief's hut, I was met by the unworldly sight of the moon and the stars streaking across the heavens like sand scattered across a dark palette. The entire village was asleep and blanketed by a celestial glow. For a long time, I stood at the door, looking up.

Then, out of the corner of my eye, I saw shadows flitting in the water. Although its surface reflected the sky, the water had become semitransparent in its light. I stepped closer to the edge of the pier to take a look and was met with the splashing of large fins. At first, what I thought I saw were large *bangus* or yellowfin teasing the surface. Hundreds of dark outlines slowly made their way in every direction under the pier and beyond. However, the more I studied them, the more their fins appeared as limbs, the more their gestures became a language.

Then, suddenly, I saw them. Beneath us was an entire village of these beings working under the water, plainly visible in the penetrating moonlight. They searched the ocean floor on two legs, swam quickly after fish, entered and exited cavernous holes in the ground, and greeted one another. Although I could see their gestures and shapes, their exact appearance and intentions were still unclear. I wanted to continue studying them, but the more I tried to look, the more my knees weakened and heart pounded. Eventually, it became too much. I backed away from the pier, hearing only the sound of my blood pumping, my staggered breathing. I crept back into the chief's hut so as not to let my absence be discovered, but you were already there, standing where I had been sleeping.

In the moonlight from the window, I noticed your glassy eyes first. They shone like two giant pearls protruding from the sand. Startled, you stood straight, revealing your tall and slender body covered in scales and gills. Your hands and feet: webbed and clawed. And your face—your face petrified me.

Where a human would have their nose, mouth, and chin, your tentacles sprawled and coiled like they had minds of their own.

Then there was the familiar smell, the one of dead fish, the pungent odor I had come to associate with Marie. Somehow, I hadn't noticed until then, but the smell had been there in the village. You had been there.

In whatever tremulous voice I could muster, I asked you if you had written the letter and if you had taken my father. You made a noise I could only understand as a chuckle. It was guttural and hoarse like when Marie tried to talk. Somehow, it put me at ease. You began to move toward the door, beckoning me with your claw. I followed, checking on the sleeping chief as I passed. He was snoring quietly.

Trembling, I watched as you peered over the water. You beckoned me again. I stood in the doorway before mustering enough courage to push myself forward. I took my place beside you and looked down. At first, I saw what I had already seen. Life went on under the sea, your people going about their lives like a silent film. But then I caught it, above the water, in the reflection of the moon and stars. The silhouette of two people gradually began to fill in. Suddenly, I saw what you had been looking at, what you had been trying to say. Beyond what I thought you were, there was something I had missed. A familiar flush in your cheek, a recognizable narrow arc above where your mouth was supposed to be, a unique and habitual twitch where your tentacles curled. We had both inherited what our parents left us. You were Dumama and I was Jokoko, but those were just names for what were practically the same. We nodded at each other and, as if confirming that I understood you, you slowly dropped back into the water, blending in with everything below and above us. I went back to bed and, in the morning, I left without saying goodbye, which was Dad's way of leaving.

♦ ♦ ♦

Somehow, I came home, but I realize now how much your invitation meant to me. Dad still hasn't come back, and I don't think he ever will. I feel like he left me a long time ago, before he even stepped off your island. I think, had he the chance, he would have taken you instead. You knew that, didn't you? You have that in common, you know? Sacrifice.

Still, I know the likelihood of this happening is low because I know how difficult it is to give up all you've ever known and loved, but on the off chance you do, on the off chance this reaches you and you find yourself wondering, if you find yourself in the States, don't hesitate to stay with me. You have family here and wherever I go. I'll be waiting.

The Price of a Miracle

"It's not too difficult to make something like this happen, don't you think?" Edwin asks me, and I say he should know since he'd gone and already done it. We're through several pints at a brewery in their outdoor patio area looking out at some train tracks running parallel and, beyond that, the city where we're from. They ring a bell when the train comes by, "they" being the employees: the servers and the barbacks and the brewers. The rumbling happens, then the whistle, then the dusty gust and heaping force that wants to pick up everything like it's got teeth, like it has a mouth to swallow the landscape whole and chew.

When the train comes, they stop what they're doing and they ring these bells they got all around the walls. Customers aren't supposed to touch them. Only they can. When you hear it, and you're sitting on the outside, you gotta hunker down, 'less you want to ruin what you paid for. You don't listen to the bells, then you only got yourself to blame.

Edwin's made twenty grand marrying a twenty-something-year-old ex-beauty queen from the Philippines for a green card. I can't believe he's done it, but he has. I fight the urge to call it a miracle because it's not. It's just fooling to be, like a flytrap fools to be anything but.

What's the opposite of a miracle, I ask him.

"Why?" he asks back, grinding his teeth at the end of his IPA.

I tell him it's because whatever it is was what he's done. He's performed something as fantastical, although in the opposite sense. Less like turning water into wine and more like dumb luck, like stepping off a cliff and walking straight across just because you didn't look down. Dumb, magical luck.

"That's not nice, and it's not magic, asshole. It's fair. It's an exchange." He's still got his phone open to her picture on the table. She's in scrubs, surrounded by our empty glasses and patients. She's not a beauty queen anymore, but everyone's still got stupid grins on around her. There's more to her. She's gone to medical school. Done the certification. Could've been a doctor except she had an easier time getting certified as a nurse in the States.

She's too smart and too beautiful for him, I tell Edwin, it's like she's trading her hands for gloves, her feet for shoes. She should stay where she is. Why America?

"I'm not asking you to ask questions. I'm asking you for answers," Edwin says, swiping her picture off the screen and disappearing the smiles. "But you're one to talk. You were born here. You don't know what it's like. People over there in the poor provinces like where she and I are from don't have anything to lose. That's a dangerous way to live. Sure, there's freedom, but freedom's just pacing back and forth in one place. Everyone dreams of getting out of there, of being more."

Edwin's words strike a nerve. He knows what I told him about my mother. How age shed the right mind from her until all she did was pace from one end of her convalescent home to the other. There was peace on her face except when you tried to get her to do anything else like eat or use the bathroom or sleep.

If I could become him, I start, and he could become me, that would be something, but I didn't finish my sentence. There was more to it at the end I was swallowing with the rest of my lager.

"If you were me, you'd still be over there," Edwin says, sunlight blinking off our glasses as cars pass. "If I was you, nothing would've changed. I would've still been in the same place as you are now, and that's the difference."

I ask Edwin what else he could give her that she hasn't already paid for and he starts flagging down the server like we're lost at sea, like his life depends on it. She comes by and she's already picking up our empties before he can ask what he wants.

"Can we get another round?" Edwin says and she sputters a "got it," already at another table.

I repeat my question, but he starts to answer it before I can finish. "She has to stay married to me at least a year. That's how these things go. In the meantime, we have to build a portfolio to share with immigration to prove we're legit. We go on trips, parties with the family, shopping, the works. Take a ton of pictures, build a story. That's where the romancing happens. That's where I can win her over."

I tell him I don't know, but it sounds risky. I tell him that if he forces too many things in that portfolio it might look suspicious. Like if you dye your hair a certain color too thoroughly it doesn't look natural. If anything, it's just telling people, especially the ones who aren't looking, you got something to hide.

"There's no great gain without great risk," he says, but I tell him his gain is his risk. I bring up the uncanny valley, and Occam's razor, and all the reasons not to be perfect, not to want more, not to pursue miracles, when the rattling brims and the bells ring. Everyone outside takes hold of their glasses but our table is barren. In one swoop, the hunk of iron bellows and screams, glasses overturning, beers spilling, people losing. And, at the end of it, the aftermath is the same as it was before. The train goes from point A to point B before where we are and where we come from, before the mountains and the valleys and the sharp horizons sunk beyond our reach.

Bellow Below

My fraternal twin's name was Boni—short for Bonifacio—and before we separated, we coleased a two-bedroom, one-and-a-half-bathroom deal in Burbank. The building was old, but the rooms had been refurbished, and the owners couldn't wait to make their money back. It was perfect timing. Boni had settled into a gig with a family e-zine writing fluff like top ten TikTok lists and how-tos for blood sugar pinpricks and Apple Pay, and me, I had a stable position in a Christian advertisement firm writing clickbait for people looking for absolution and KY Jelly. In other words, we were fresh scum ready to migrate from our primordial ooze/parent's house and strike out on our own, together. We applied and signed the lease the next day. We didn't have to look at what we were getting into. We were free, and that's all we wanted.

Boni and I were as close as twins could get, but it wasn't without its pains. We grew up in the same tract house with the same immigrant-exiled parents, the same Catholic school classes with the same hard-fought grades, the same discount-designer clothes with the same knock-off BOGO shoes, but despite all that, we were completely different. Boni was the more demonstrative one. He wasn't without friends. But the same could be said about enemies, and he made a lot of them. Yet there was always some delight he took in seeing people upset and spiteful. Some delight he had even in his own feelings and reactions to things. He had girlfriends through grade school then switched to boyfriends in college. He never held relationships for long and it was seldom I ever met a partner.

I, on the other hand, was always the more reserved one. I kept my dislikes to myself and chose the least abrasive form of opposition to whatever challenges I met. I made few friends and have dated only three guys in my entire life, sleeping with the second only once after four years of prodding, and eventually marrying the third. Nevertheless, it was all to the same merit as my brother: I took pleasure in knowing these experiences, be it joy and pain, happiness and sorrow, gain and loss. It didn't matter whose: theirs or mine.

Despite our differences, Boni and I reveled in these interactions together and told each other everything. Not just our everythings about others but also our everythings about ourselves. I knew how he wanted to tear out Abigail Legaspi's hair when she kissed him in sixth grade, and he knew how I threw away my panties so our mom wouldn't find out I slept with my second boyfriend when she did the family laundry. You learn more about a person when you hear what they think about other people. Boni and I knew each other more than anyone else, which was probably the start of our inevitable unraveling. Like a trapeze act where you have to trust the person to catch you and hold you and know when to let you go, we were the perfect pair. We really knew how to say goodbye.

And it all began when I told him about my future husband. It was two years into us living together, and Boni suspected what I was going to tell him the moment I invited him to the new expensive contemporary restaurant by our house, but he didn't mention his suspicions until he was already there, talking about the *bangus* we had both ordered—or milkfish, the waiter had called it in his jubilant recitation of "today's specials."

"Milkfish caught just a few days ago from the volcanic coast of Tagaytay?" Boni mimicked the way our waiter orated the script, smiling like the Cheshire Cat from Wonderland except he couldn't turn invisible even if he tried, "I wonder if it came in a balikbayan box with a couple of souvenirs? A T-shirt? No, a cute barrel-man! I'd love to pull up one—"

Afraid someone might hear him condescending the restaurant, I tacitly kicked him and told him to behave.

"It's *bangus*," he uttered more softly but with more pomp, "why not call it what it is?"

"It's milkfish. That's what it's called."

"No, it's called *bangus* in the Philippines. It's called *awa awa* in Hawaii, *ikan susu* in Malaysia. It's *bangus*. You can Google it."

"It's all milkfish. Google *that*."

"God, we can get this any time at a tenth of the price."

"Then why did you order it?"

"I'm curious why it's the same price as the Wagyu skirt steak. Oh, I'm sorry, *beef* skirt steak. Maybe it has something to do with the volcano? Will there be shards of obsidian, you think?"

Unamused, I ignored his joke, and we quietly drank our twelve-dollar domestic beers until our food arrived. With the glow of a proud parent, our waiter delicately placed both plates before us at the same time. In the center of each, a six-ounce, skin-on, square fillet of *bangus* rested over a bed of black currant, mungo bean, and a bright orange puree of butternut squash and spices. Dashed around the plate were two spoon-waves of green chimichurri and four sprigs of fennel. The familiar pungent smell of the fish frying in our parent's kitchen mingled with the austere and delicate aromatics of the restaurant's interpretation. Our minds wandered back and forth between familiar and unfamiliar territory and, for a moment, I thought we might get to enjoy our meal after all the doubt, but the waiter wasn't done with his service.

"Cane-na! Enjoy."

Boni and I shuddered. We both knew what he had tried to say, but I was hoping to be wrong while Boni was hoping to be right when we asked him to repeat what he said.

"Cane-na. It means, 'come eat with us' in the Tagalog."

"We know. We're Filipino. It's *ka-in-na*." Boni mouthed each word slowly, sticking out his tongue for the "ka" and "na" and flashing all his teeth with the "in."

"Ka-ina?"

"*Ka-in-na*."

"Kayina?"

"*Ka-in-na!*"

The waiter and Boni went back and forth, each attempt getting more ridiculously exaggerated in speech until it sounded more like a Haka war cry than an invitation to dinner. After startling a few tables around us and what seemed like a hundred *kain na*s, Boni finally stopped torturing the poor guy.

"There! You got it!" Boni exclaimed, giving the waiter a high-five.

Feeling accomplished, the waiter barked "*kain na*" once more before gleefully meeting his next guests.

"You're an ass," I whispered. We didn't even speak the language ourselves, let alone know whether or not someone was pronouncing something the right way.

Nevertheless, Boni was pleased with himself. He lifted a fork and turned his teasing from the waiter to his meal. "Well, at least he could say Tagaytay and Tagalog." The brittle skin made a satisfying crackling sound as his fork sliced easily through it and the plump white meat. I broke into my own and we both mouthed a piece at the same time. Savoring the delicate flavors, I tried to meditate on the taste but was disrupted by Boni's immediate sigh of disapproval. Like a heavy cloud of gloom, his groan withered whatever hopes may have been incubating on my tongue. Neither of us took another bite.

"It's not that bad. We should eat it," I said, not willing to give up so easily.

"Go ahead. I'm sending this back."

"Really? It's a goddamn new restaurant, Boni! Be nice! You've been rude ever since we got here!" I said and, upon hearing my voice rise, proceeded to fork another piece of *bangus*, unable to taste it through my anger and anticipation of what I needed to say.

"Ok, I've been rude. I'm sorry. But come on, this *bangus*, it's not worth as much as that Wagyu."

"That's not the point," I said but agreed. No matter how good this dish was, Wagyu was always going to be better than *bangus*. "The point is that you need to stop criticizing people so readily and condescending them with your sleazy, bourgeois attitude."

"But they started it," he whined, play-pouting like a child.

"Don't do that to me. I deserve better from you."

He settled back in his seat. "*Susmariosep*. You sound like Mom when she found me in bed with the choirmaster."

"Is everything a joke to you?"

"Do you have to eat everything you pay for?"

"You're hurting people, Boni. Some people are too stupid to see you do it to them. Some people even think it's cool. But you won't be able to live like this forever. Eventually you're going to have to grow up."

"Something tells me this isn't about *bangus*," he said, picking up his drink and rubbing his upper lip on its brim.

"Unbelievable. This is why you don't have a steady boyfriend."

"I have a boyfriend, thank you very much."

"No, you have boy toys. You don't have relationships, you play games. When are you going to get serious? When are you going to start showing some self-control and start trusting people enough to enjoy what's good about them?"

"And you're telling me you've grown up?"

"Yeah, I have. I met a guy." I finally confessed and told him about number three. He nodded silently, drinking his beer while I told him about how we met and how long we had been seeing each other and how I thought it was getting serious. Boni had stopped talking, already getting out of me what he needed to hear. It was the first time I had kept something from him. Had someone eavesdropped on us, they may have mistaken me for someone admitting to an affair, but they wouldn't be wrong. I was cheating on my partner, betraying his trust for my own benefit under the delusion of saving his feelings. What made it worse was Boni wouldn't even think of doing the same thing to me. Despite all his failings—his pageantry and sadistic ways—he would never try to lie or intentionally hurt me. Soon after, we boxed the *bangus*, left a tip, and kept our leftovers until they started to smell like fruit and cheese.

The third guy's name was Boying Bautista, but everyone called him Boy. Every Filipino family has an Uncle Boy, but I never thought I'd ever meet one my age, let alone date and marry them. Boy was an engineer for a private military contractor, the kind that required family interviews and security clearance to get through the door. He was always trying to fix things. The first time I visited his apartment, there were gutted appliances and their miscellaneous parts strewn across his floor. The only place that was untouched by the clutter was the kitchen. He was always trying to take broken things apart and learn how to repurpose their pieces to help other things work. He didn't like to waste anything. Other than that, everything else about him was unremarkable, and I knew it would be hard to get Boni to like him, to justify my hiding Boy from him without further compromising my personal choices and interests.

But the more Boy and I stayed together, the more I became critical of Boni. In our twenty-five years of living together, the most dependable thing about Boni was that he wasn't. Sometimes he would give you his full attention, shower you with all the understanding, wit, and praise you'd ever want from anyone in your life. Then, the other times, he would ignore you, your thoughts and feelings, or worse: discard them without giving you a second thought. He tortured people, whether on purpose or not, in favor of his own pleasure. It's what attracted people to him. Boy was the opposite of that. He rather torture himself than waste anyone's feelings. It was pitiful but endearing. It was something Boni could never offer.

Before I asked Boni to meet Boy in person, I shared a picture of him on my phone like a psychologist trying to mentally prepare their patient to reexperience a traumatic episode. By that time, Boni had listened to me talk about Boy, but he never asked after him. I felt the need to push things forward and went to the last picture Boy and I had taken together on my phone. I was sure Boni had seen it on my social media, but he never reacted or commented on anything I ever posted there.

Boni rested his back on the floor of our apartment, holding up my phone above his face. I rested on the couch. In the picture, Boy and I were each holding opposite ends of a narwhal tusk at Fisherman's Wharf.

"Cute teeth."

"Shut up."

"Didn't they use a narwhal tusk to beat up that London Bridge loon?"

"Stop holding my phone that way. You'll drop it on your face."

Boni turned his back to me and swiped through more of my pictures of Boy and me on my phone. "Why are you showing me these?"

"I didn't know if you've seen him before."

"I have. Not my type."

"I don't care if he is. Not everybody likes the same things you do, you know."

He continued through, going further and further back in time. He slowed at a picture of Boy drilling a post to the beam of a gazebo at his parent's house. In another picture, his father and him were fastening a guardrail in place. Another one, his mother and I mixing cement.

"You met his parents?"

"Yeah, so? Boy's really close to them. They're not like us. They and Boy came here when he was ten."

"So he's a FOB?"

"No, he speaks English pretty well. You wouldn't know he was from over there from just listening to him."

"Never thought he was the type to get his hands dirty. Color me impressed." He swiped back to Boy drilling. "Look at those biceps. Why are you showing me this again?"

"Well," I hesitated, sitting up from the couch. I crossed my legs and pinched my thighs, hoping to spur the words forward. "I was hoping to invite him here for dinner, just the three of us."

"You want me to meet him?"

"Yeah, and I want him to meet you."

"Has he met Mom and Dad?"

"Of course not. I mean, eventually. But I really want you two to know each other."

"We do. We know *of* each other, right?"

"Come on!"

"So, this is it, huh?" Boni sat up and tossed my phone beside me on the couch. He stretched his arms up.

"Yeah, this is it."

"He propose already?"

"We just talked about it. He didn't do the knee thing yet."

"No knee thing? Boo. Call me old-fashioned, but grand gestures need to make a comeback, pronto. What I wouldn't give to have Ryan Gosling just sweep me up in the rain and make my brown ass feel safe."

"They never went away. It'll probably still happen that way when it becomes official, sans the Ryan Gosling part. It's just, I don't know."

"I know," he said, then got up for a quick shower, dressed, and left for a date before I could climb off the couch.

The next day, my parents FaceTimed me at work an hour before a staff meeting.

"Did he tell you?" I asked, typing while I talked. My phone leaned on a picture frame I had of Boni and I as kids sliding down a snow slope in a green plastic toboggan. He was behind me, holding the reins.

"Not outright. You know how he is," my mom said, sitting beside Dad. They knew secrets better than anyone. In the Philippines, they had served the Marcos family and even helped Imelda Marcos and her shoe collection escape to Hawaii. Although they weren't allowed to return home since, they were well compensated for their loyalty. They survived on secrets; theirs and others.

"I didn't tell him to tell you guys. I was going to eventually tell you on my own."

"We know, *nakong*," my father said, his stomach protruding from under his shirt, "you don't need to tell us about him yet."

I stopped typing and sighed at them on my phone. "He's a year younger than I am and an engineer. He and his family are from Sorsogon City."

"Ah, good," my mom chimed, "He's a Pinoy! Thank God. Does he live with his parents?"

"No, his own place."

"A house?"

"An apartment."

"Catholic?" my dad asked.

"Goes to church with his family every Sunday."

"Good."

"Is that all?"

"You just let us know when we can meet him, *nakong*. You shouldn't hide things from us. We're your family."

"I wasn't, but I will plan something for us in the future."

"Look at your brother. He's *bakla* but we still love him."

"I love him too," I said and went to my meeting and about the rest of my week, a call a day from them with the same affirmations and the same exchange of words. It got to the point where I couldn't tell who was being vetted anymore: Boy, Boni, or myself.

Finally, the day came. Boy arrived for dinner half an hour early, bringing an unexpected gift. In his hands were cans of coconut milk, premade purple balls of mochiko, and a bag of uncooked, rainbow-colored tapioca.

"What's this?" I asked, already helping him put down what he brought in the kitchen. Boni's Greek salad was chopped and kept ready to be served from the same Tupperware container it was shaken in, but my Stouffer's lasagna was still frozen and needed another hour.

Boy looked in the oven window and I felt a twinge of embarrassment rise up my neck about how cheap and lazy a ready-made lasagna made me look.

"I thought I'd make you two some of my classic *bilo-bilo* for dessert," he said, rising from the oven door.

I took him in for a kiss and held him close at the waist even though I knew it didn't make him feel comfortable for me to take the lead. He was conservative that way. "How thoughtful. I love that stuff."

He quickly held me in turn, trying not to let me get the better of him. "I just need a pot. Where is Boni?"

I frowned in his arms. "Still getting ready."

"Did someone say pot?" Boni suddenly interrupted, sliding into view with nothing but his dress shirt, boxers (thank God), and socks on.

Angered and embarrassed, I jerked away from Boy and confronted him. "You fucking asshole!"

Boni ignored me. "Sorry, I'm Boni still-getting-ready. Charmed."

Afraid to see Boy's face, I didn't turn around until I heard him clap and whistle. "All right! Awesome, man! *Jerry Maguire*?"

I was simultaneously taken aback and relieved.

Boni smirked. "*Risky Business*," he said, and walked over to shake Boy's hand.

"I'm Boying. Boy for short."

"You got an old man's name."

"I know. It's ironic, isn't it? Old Boy."

"And an oxymoron."

"What? Oh, yeah. I guess my full name does sound like a spring. Boing, boing."

"No, that's onomatopoeia."

"On a what?"

Boni turned to me, his smile trembling, half-naked, finally feeling like the most absurd one in the room. "Nice teeth," he murmured and walked back to his lair.

"Thanks, man!" Boy said after him. "Invisalign!"

The rest of the time Boni was gone, I sat back and watched Boying and the oven cook. He prepared the tapioca balls first and let them cool in a bowl of cold water while he let the coconut milk come to a boil. When the milk started bubbling, he put in the purple mochiko balls, followed by the tapioca. Finally, he stirred in a cup of sugar and let the whole thing simmer. That was all there was to it. Watching him make it for me in his kitchen the first time helped me understand him better. I worried that what I saw thawing in the oven would give him the wrong impression of me, but when it was done and on the table, the lasagna was just a lasagna to him. I realize now that's why I loved him.

By the time the table was set, Boni was back. He took his seat at the head of the table with Boy and I on each side. Properly dressed now, to my surprise.

"There he is," Boy said, already helping himself to the lasagna.

"Here I am," Boni replied, opening a can of beer he brought from the kitchen.

Listening to its snap and hiss, I immediately wanted one

too, but before I could get up, Boni was already calling from the kitchen. "Sorry, I forgot to bring you beers too."

"Wow, thanks, bro!" Boy exclaimed with glee, piling extra feta onto his Greek salad.

I saw Boni pause at the mention of "bro," but continue back with the beers. He placed one down in front of me and then the other in front of Boy before taking his seat again. He held his beer but didn't drink it. I was surprised by his show of restraint. "Someone make *bilo-bilo*?"

"Yup, my personal recipe." Boy said, sprinkling a generous helping of parmesan on his lasagna. He wasn't shy. He ate ravenously as he talked.

"Funny, I lifted the lid and I didn't see anything in it. Just the mochiko and tapioca."

Boy laughed, wiping his chin with the back of one hand while he lifted more lettuce with the other. "And ube and coconut milk."

"Yeah, that's it. It's purple."

"That's not nothing."

I could tell Boni wanted to say more, but he drank his beer instead.

Boy, on the other hand, chewed while talking and opening his beer. I had never heard him talk so much before that night. "I know it's strange. Sorry. You expected more in there, right? It's my own recipe. Boy's *bilo-bilo*." He took a sip of his beer and looked down at the food on the table before continuing. "Growing up, we didn't have a lot of anything. But a couple of times a year, my wealthy Auntie Jessa in the States would send us money, and the whole family would splurge on food. I remember the first things my parents would buy were ingredients for *bilo-bilo*. There'd be fresh bananas, camote, ube, buko cubes, and fresh jackfruit, but despite all those fancy ingredients, the only thing that mattered to me were the cheapest parts. My grandparents and all the kids would roll the mochiko balls with grated ube all night and let them sit until they were ready to cook in the morning. The tapioca balls came in a large pack you just had to microwave with water, and there was so much of it the other kids and I would throw them at each other and make the adults run after us with bullwhips.

"When it all cooked together and everything was done, all I ever did was pick out everything except for what's in the pot today. I know it's childish, but all that other stuff is just extra, right? It's still *bilo-bilo*."

I looked at Boni, and for the first time he didn't have that stupid grin on his face whenever he wanted to play with someone. Instead, he listened with something else. "Well, it's not called balls for nothing. Or is it balls-balls?"

"You gotta have two! One ball is not enough! It's *bilo-bilo*, not *bilo*!" Boy said and the two of them shared a hearty laugh. By the time Boy was finished with his first plate, both our plates were still empty.

And when the dinner was over and Boy had left, a strange emptiness still lingered in both of us that we didn't want to acknowledge, hoping it would go away on its own like a cat bellowing in the night.

"Thanks for being nice," I yawned, already in my pajamas.

Boni was still in the living room, still completely dressed and reading a book. "You're welcome."

"Staying up?"

"Staying up. Not done yet."

"So, what do you think?"

Boni exhaled and put his book aside. I couldn't see the cover, but I could tell it was something new. He was always reading the new stuff. "He's got balls."

I laughed and took my place next to him, leaning my head on his shoulder. "There you are."

"Here I am."

"No, but really."

"He's great. I'm happy for you. Really."

"He's not boring?"

"He's a little boring."

"I knew it. You hate him."

"I don't. It's just." He put his arm around me and kissed my forehead, holding me tight. "Is this really it? Are you sure?"

I closed my eyes and buried my head deeper into his chest. Searching for an answer, thundering in the darkness there below, it was easy to mistake his heartbeat for mine.

After Bigfoot

I had not spoken with my sister Mari in more than a year when her text box cascaded down my home screen, draping over the face of our father, who had died the year before.

"*Kamusta ka,* Kuya? How're you doin'?" the first text read. Before I could reply, my father's head was replaced by two more texts. "Know anything about Bigfeet?" "*Bigfoot."

I swiped our father away with my thumb. "I know the two but not the one." "Hahaha," my sister replied. "If those were the problem I'd just need the right shoes."

"Hahaha." Neither one of us was into LOLs.

"4real, Kuya. I saw it. Dad was right. It's here."

Although I already understood her, I still didn't want to believe it, so my thumbs played dumb. "Right foot or left foot?" I texted.

For a long time, she didn't reply, and the sudden illogical dread overtook me that I would never read another word from her again.

My father's heart attack brought us together. Me, his son, and her, his estranged daughter, my half sister from a country he traded for another. He came to the United States for Mari and her mother, but little did they know, their happy lives would be apart. Her mother married the village Albularyo, my father married a fellow nurse, had me, and we all lived happily ever after for a while. My parents sent them money. They sent us pounds of *cornick* and *butong pakwan* and healing leaves from rainbow eucalyptus in return. Pictures were exchanged. Mari told me she watched me grow above their altar. I told her I watched her grow on my refrigerator. I used to look up to that familiar stranger whose similarities to myself only deepened with time, like how the tide can uncover debris, and how it can bury all the steps that took it there.

When Mari finally texted back, I was out for my evening jog. Siri's monotone voice rattled into my headphones while Gary Wright's "Dream Weaver" and the heavy clops of my tired feet beat in rhythm.

"Sister-said-you-should-come-visit-Koo-YEAH," Siri dribbled into my ear, "do-you-want-to-reply?"

I stopped and sucked in a cold, painful breath, then took my phone from its arm strap and brushed our father away again.

"I can't really take any time off work. Maybe summer?"

"Always summer *nalang*. You either come now or not at all."

I read the block of text running down my screen. The choppy guitar of "This Is It" led into Kenny Loggins's raspy falsetto by the time I figured out how to reply.

"Hahaha."

"He won't be here for long."

"Who?"

"Bigfoot *tangina*."

"Bigfoot. Sorry." I waited, a cold gust biting my wet back.

"So are you coming?"

"Can't I wait for him to come back. To come to me?"

"He's not from where you are. Who knows where he'll go next."

I thought of my father, and for the first time since his funeral I wished he was still alive in my place. It didn't matter to me if I saw him. It didn't matter to me if he existed or not.

"Is next week too late?"

"I'll ask him."

By the time she replied that he would still be there, I had already walked the mile home.

I was raised in a house where the less you said, the better. If you didn't talk about a problem, it didn't become one. I never asked about the people in the Philippines or the girl who looked like me, and my father never talked about them.

The only thing that my father talked on and on about was Bigfoot, and it was hard to call it anything but a problem. Ok, maybe less a problem and more of an obsession. On the outside, my father looked like a model nurse and family man. Hospitable and knowledgeable to his colleagues and patients, kind and loving to his wife and his son. However, my father's world was inhabited by conspiracy radio, tin-foil hats, and top-tens of grainy YouTube videos of the unexplainable and supposedly supernatural.

In his spare time, especially in his retirement, he studied the obscure and unsolved mysteries in the world. Days before he passed away, he obsessed over the figure from his childhood, the most well-known of the cryptids, the one I thought could never be caught outside of the Americas.

"I saw him once in the Philippines," he said, shuffling through old papers on the couch while my mother tried to figure out how to fill out the last corner of her sudoku at their dining table.

"The Philippines? Like the Rock Apes in Vietnam?"

"No, no." He spat into faded clippings of men in monster suits, dead trees with people's faces in them. "It was Bigfoot. The Sasquatch. He was real big and real hairy and real brown and real human-looking except for his arms and legs." He parroted the gesture of Bigfoot's famous picture. One arm was in front and the other behind while he was sitting down, like he was the top half of the man in all the walk signs.

"Why was he in the Philippines?"

"*Hindi ko alam*. I don't know. Maybe he likes it there. Maybe vacation."

"What was he doing?"

"What else? He was just walking round, trying not to be seen, hiding in trees. *Pagpunta dito at doon*."

"Leaving footprints, saving little girls, and checking on the Hendersons?"

"*Susmariosep*. Serious *ako*. I saw him with my two eyes."

"What did you do?"

"What else is there to do? *Tumakbo ako!* I ran!"

◆ ◆ ◆

After our texts, I left that Monday in April on the first ticket I could find. I had never been to the Philippines, and I neglected to notice the seventeen-hour flight duration listed on my boarding pass until I was well past TSA at the International Terminal at LAX. It was my first time flying and my stomach had been doing somersaults since the night before. In my initial shock, I walked to the gate in my socks, my sneakers still in hand.

Eight hours, three barf bags, two soiled pillows, and four shirt changes later, I had finally settled into my economy seat squished between the window and an obese Filipino couple.

"It happens to the best of us," the husband beside me said,

his arm well into my personal space, his flaps of excess elbow skin curled between my arm and my rib. I smiled, smelling my old bile settled behind my teeth and feeling the rest ebb up and down in my throat.

After another ten hours, I awoke at last to the captain announcing our descent. Below, lines of smoke and dots of fire covered the emerald landscape. The plane quivered down and bounced at the landing, but I was alive. I was finally there.

Before I could get a sense of the ground under my feet, I was pushed through customs and into the wide, humid berth of this new country. Immediately, I was swarmed by a dozen valets calling me sir and asking to carry my one roller bag to their taxi. In the mass of reaching arms, I saw my name written on cardboard, held at waist-level by a thin man leaning on a maroon van. I apologized to my welcoming committee as I made my way to my ride: a man no less than a decade older than me with barely a hair on his long, naked legs. The driver only took notice of me when I was right in front of him.

"Hello. Did Mari send you?"

The man squinted, his eyes like two puckering lips. He brought the sign down and leaned closer, his head almost to my chin. "*Ano?*"

I stepped back and tried to recollect what Tagalog I knew. "Uh, Kili-lala Mari?"

The man looked up at my face and revealed a surprisingly

pristine set of teeth. I looked away, catching the valets from before swarm another set of people leaving the airport. "*Ito ay ki-lala.*"

"I'm sorry, I don't understand."

"It's ok lang. I especk English-English po." He winked up at me and took my bag. I watched him roll it to his side and begin opening the sliding door to his van.

"So you know Mari?"

"*Oo naman.* He paid me to pick you up and dribe you po, ok?" He put his back to me and brought my bag up and in the back seat.

"She, you mean."

"*Aye, tanga,* a-SHE. Sorry *na* po. Let's go, *tara na!*" He stepped aside to let me in.

I walked beside him and put one foot up before I stopped. I held out my hand. "I'm sorry, what's your name?"

"*Ako?* Amado Veracrus po. Nice to meet you po," he said and shook my hand vigorously.

"Nice to meet you, Amado," I said and took my hand away from him before he broke my wrist. I climbed in and fastened my belt while Amado closed the door and walked around to his driver's seat. I watched him fidget with his rearview mirror before he started the engine, its low, healthy hum immediately flushing the car with cool air.

"Amado?" I asked, and when he ignored me, I said it louder. "Amado?"

He shook in surprise. "Ah, sorry po. Do you need anything po?"

"Are you hard of hearing?"

"Sorry po. My ears do not work good. No good *ngayon na*."

"That's ok. What time do you think we'll get there?"

Amado lifted his gold watch to his face. After a while, he held it out to me. "*Tangina!* What does dot say na?"

I looked at the watch, the face of the clock scratched up but still visible. "It's ten thirty-five."

"Sorry po. My eyes do not work good needer! But do-not-warry po. I drive good neberdaless na!"

I smiled, a cold line running down my back and to my quivering knees as the van pulled onto the expressway out of the airport.

The roads in the Philippines were menacing to say the least, and for once, it made me miss LA traffic. Bumper to bumper, I once saw a man asleep at the wheel beside me. Afraid for his life, I honked my horn to wake him up and inadvertently startled the Tesla in front of me, propelling him into an expensive-looking camper. The guilt from that time resurfaced the moment Amado and I got on the road. The streets of Manila were crowded, and yet its cars maneuvered them at incredible speeds. The wheels swayed from the lines that guided them, limbs dangled from jeepneys like the thick hairs of stampeding woolly mammoths, and the stoplights did very little of what was intended of them. Each intersection was a magical slam dance of almost-accidents. Through the windshield of the man driving around us from the left, I saw the light of a movie playing on a tablet on his dash, and through the truck pushing forward from our right, the devilish glitter of messages being received, eager hands returning heart and prayer emojis, their palms effortlessly steering his course.

And just when I thought the buildings and people and cars would smother us for the entirety of our journey, the road broke into wide green seas of grass and farmland, the city sucked into the smog-smeared horizon behind us. Speckles of carabao and pigs dotted the landscape while the homes hid and smoldered behind domes of leafy plumes. The straight roads led into turns and the turns led down into thick wood and wetter terrain. We only stopped once, to get gas from a station that also sold *parols*. I stepped out, too distracted by the array of circles and paper-star symmetry to avoid the frogs that covered the ground. Three twitched under my sneakers, ruined by my carelessness, another stayed limp but warm under the ball of my right foot.

Pathetically, I danced my way to the cashier and his stars, hopping from one frog to the next, a blather of flat amphibians in my wake, until I met him, smiling. Myself, diminished, sad.

"*Amerikano ka ba?*" he said, handing me my newly purchased *parol* draped in newspaper, a frog jumping up and off the counter.

"What gave it away?" I asked, looking at his bare feet, red without remorse.

He pointed with one of his big toes at my soiled shoe. "You still care."

A week before our father's funeral, Mari arrived in LA. What stood out to me the most about her was her impeccable posture and incredibly large hands. I bowed before her and lifted the weight of one to my forehead before she snatched it away and whacked my arm with the other. "*Bastos!*" she said. Her first words to me ever.

Mari was my elder by five years, and by custom and culture, I was supposed to refer to her as my *Ate* and greet her with the same respect any Filipino greets their older relative: the plaintive yet intimate kiss on the back of the hand with the younger relative's forehead. However, Mari and other Filipino women like her disliked the practice and preferred designating others the reflexive terms. The elder became the younger, the *Ate* became the *Nene*, and the *Totoy* (I, the younger brother) became the *Kuya* (older, and less youthful). It was an exchange of words that only siphoned the life from those who cared.

"Kuya," she called me and took me in her arms. She was shorter than me, but I fell into her easily.

That week, we got to know each other. I told her about my life thus far and our father's obsession with the bizarre, and she told me about the home he left, the people she helped, her mother and stepfather. Like the father we had in common, she left home to attend medical school and fell in love, but it was not far enough to keep her away, and the love not deep enough to make her forget. She returned to her family and brought with her all she learned. Eventually, her mother and stepfather passed away without me knowing. Eventually, she became the sole person the village depended on and settled into her own solitary life, the one she had always lived apart from my father and me.

"These big hands I got from my mother," she explained, gripping a cold mug of tea. We had talked for hours by then. "My *ama-ama*, my other father, he loved her because of these hands. She could hold so much water."

I looked into my mug, empty from my lack of words. "What does that mean?"

"*Ano?* What does what mean?"

"Holding so much water?"

Mari smiled, an edge to her lip the same as my father's, the same as mine. "*Walang* meaning, Kuya. It's just what it is. She could hold a lot. It's very useful."

We shared a laugh as the light fell, time moving faster between us, as if it were trying to make up or compensate for the distance that had kept us apart.

"Well, I don't know anything about big hands, but I can tell you about Bigfoot."

"Swollen foot? Like edema? You just need to keep active, Kuya. Jog or walk regularly."

"No, I mean Bigfoot the creature," I explained and began going into it and Dad's history. The run-ins and snapshots in America. The websites and Dad's obsession. The one occurrence he wouldn't let go of or deny. By the time I finished talking, all the light was gone, and we were nothing but silhouettes of ourselves draped on the walls.

Mari's large hand engulfed her cup. In the dark, it appeared as if she were holding the mug upside down, trapping something inside. As if what hid underneath could easily show through the cup and her hands if she wasn't careful. "If you think about it, if Bigfoot exists, anything is possible, *diba*?"

I felt my fingers and imagined water running through them, falling away and into a stream. "Yeah, but why the Philippines? I don't think the climate agrees with his fur."

Mari let go of her mug, raised her hands, stretched, and yawned. Above her, they domed like an umbrella. At my father's funeral, neither one of us looked past his casket. "I guess we'll just have to find him and ask."

By the time our van came to a halt, we were fully engulfed in bark and leaf, in jagged browns and fluttered greens. The wheels eased at the crunch of dirt and sand and I did not notice the ocean until Amado opened my door and let the loud roar of waves and the buzz of sea breeze scuttle through the fringe foliage and into the dark, tinted crevice of my back seat.

Amado took my bag and let it down. I watched my step as I got out, making sure nothing was squirming under my feet. Amado shook my hand, drove his van around me, and was gone. I was alone, the light of the coast shining through the thick mass of life in front of me.

"Kuya!" Mari said from an opening beside where the coast beckoned.

I dragged my roller bag to her, its wheels clogged in leaves and grit, and fell into her embrace. She wore a soft white shirt and jean shorts. Her large hands felt my back and I imagined them texting and stumbling between messages on her phone, each finger overlapping letters several times until she got the words right. It was only then that I thought of why I was there and who I was supposed to meet. Mechanically, I handed her the *parol*, the newspaper ruffling in the wind.

"Thank you! How was the trip?"

"Long. But I'm alive. Ruined my shoes though," I said and lifted a sullied foot, the frog guts now caked in sandy mush.

"*Tae ng baka?* You step in shit?"

"Frogs."

"Frogs. *Susmariosep*. You think they would be fast enough to jump out of the way."

"They were fast. There were just too many of them."

Mari patted my back then started toward the trail. She held the *parol* before us like a lantern swinging at her fingertips. "Come on now. I can get you new shoes."

We trudged a few minutes through the trail of overgrowth, Mari pulling a branch away at points as if she were holding doors open, the wheels of my roller getting caught in a root or a vine, the star wrapped in newspaper dodging through foliage until we made it to her village. It was smaller than I expected, a dozen shacks of metal roofs and bamboo beams. The ocean masked most of what smells came from lack of plumbing and running water, but there was a constant dull odor I could only understand as decay and smoke.

The villagers did not look bothered or interested by my arrival. An old man with one eye brandished a yellow smile at us on the path and a plump woman hummed "Don't Stop Believin'" while bathing her naked child in a kiddie pool. In an open doorway (they were all open doorways), three people slept on a straw *banig*, their backs turned to me, their rear ends exposed and aimed at a large, battery-operated fan by their window. Life went on as usual.

We entered a shed closest to the path down to the beach and found a pile of shoes inside. They were of mixed sizes and tied together by the laces so the pairs didn't get separated. Mari hung the *parol* on a nail above a window, then began rummaging through them.

"What size are you?"

"Ten. What are these?"

She tossed aside a pair of women's running shoes and a pair of heavy looking dress shoes. "These are all the extra shoes we have. Most of them are too big for any of us."

I picked up a pair of Chucks and then a couple of Nikes. Adidas and Skechers rolled down at our feet. "Why are there so many?"

"People keep asking for shoes, but they keep getting sent the wrong size. Always happens. It's ok. We get what we get. We keep it for when we can use it, *nanaman*."

I looked into the soles of a pair of high heels, then at the red ones of a pair of baby shoes. "So is he still here?"

"Yeah, he's at the beach."

"What's he like?"

"He's ok. Ten, right?"

"Yeah. What do you mean ok?"

"I mean, he's not bad."

"But he's not good?"

"*Tangina*, good, bad. It doesn't matter. He's here."

"But why is he here? Did he do anything to you?"

"No, no. I just found him. He's just here."

"Bigfoot."

"Bigfoot, *talaga*!" she said and held out the perfect pair for me in her enormous hands.

He was smaller than I expected. His arms and legs looked like those of a brown gorilla, hairy and leathery and big like my father had described, but his torso was smooth and toned and thin like a model from a perfume ad. At his waist, he wore neon-green swim trunks bulging from all the air and whatever else he packed in there. His head was exactly like how it was drawn and described in all the witness descriptions and firsthand accounts. However, here his hair was combed straight and reeked of essential oils. His eyes disappeared behind wide Gucci sunglasses. And his smile looked more human than monster.

Reclining before me in his beach chair, his legs straight out, his giant feet, the only thing that really met my expectations, waved at me dandily. Upon my arrival, he leaned forward and reached for his beach umbrella.

"Where's Mar-Mar?" he said as I stopped just shy of his shade. His voice was light and kind.

"She's seeing about a sick kid," I said, although I did not know if it was true or not. Somehow, there was something in the way that she smiled before handing me the Reeboks and leading me to the beach that reminded me of my father when he talked about home. When he was avoiding things that only became worse the more you ignored them, that showed up at your door at the worst of times.

"Oh, good on her! Please, have a seat. The sand's nice and cool over here. It's been under the umbrella."

I came closer as he adjusted the umbrella over us. Upon closer inspection, his arms and legs were no bigger than mine, just hairier.

He planted the umbrella in the sand and folded his feet in. "You could get closer. I won't bite. I don't do that kind of thing."

I looked around the ground and carefully sat a foot away from him. "Thanks."

"No problem, my dude. So, what brings you to the peens?"

My ears burned at the word "peens." "I'm sure Mari told you about our father."

"Yeah, sure, sure," he said, his arms up now, his hands cupping his resting bed of hair. "Real sorry he couldn't be here. Wish I met the guy."

"I guess I just wanted to see what the big deal was?"

Bigfoot let out an unnatural giggle of glee. "Now, now! I wouldn't call myself a big deal. It's a lot of hype but I stay Hashtag-Humble. You know what I mean?"

I nodded. What should have been terror and awe overwhelming me was, instead, an uncomfortable gloss of annoyance. "Yeah."

"I am just who I am, like you're just who you are. I've been around long enough to tell you that. I've lived through empires, wars, and all sorts of civilizations. Seen black and white turn to color, life before and after Google. I can tell you things. Just ask. Whatever you want to know."

I looked at his feet. Calloused and worn from years, centuries of travel, they had taken on a stone-like, impenetrable sheen. Despite the fanfare and disappointment, he was who he claimed to be. I thought about what I could possibly ask but there wasn't really anything I wanted to know. The one who had all the questions was long gone. My father had raised me as his surrogate, but this was still not my world.

"I just got one real question, really."

"Shoot."

"Why are you here?"

"Isn't that the question for all of us, man?"

"No, shut up. I mean, why are you in the Philippines? You don't belong here!"

For a while, he didn't respond. The sea masked our breath, our heartbeats, and even our thoughts. There was no way we could reach each other without intending to, without someone taking the first step.

"Listen, you don't belong here any more than I do. Does there really need to be a reason to be anywhere? The natives, your sister, they aren't really looking for me. They know what's there. And what shouldn't be . . . that'll take care of itself, you know what I mean?"

I still talk to Mari sometimes, now and then. A text every

month. Once, I wrote that I'd come to her wedding, but she knew better than to reply. Better to let messages like that die. The ones that'll take too long to type out before the next one comes in. The ones you can't return.

For things like that, pictures were better to exchange. The Christmas after Bigfoot, we swapped pictures of our *parols*. Mine: our father's old hand-me-down. Mari's: the one I gave her. Both pictures came out as blurs that didn't look anything like stars at all, but I think they said everything we wanted them to. More than we ever could.

Handog

My father and I hadn't been talking for over a year when he passed away from COVID-19.

Perhaps his more accurate cause of death was his on-and-off-again-waste-of-one-*talagang*-hospital-visit pneumonia he liked to tease with his night walks, especially on rainy days, coupled with his irreverent chain-smoking and drinking that "*pissed-out*" instead "*pissed-off*" my mother. Every morning, without fail, he watched himself drink and smoke in the bathroom mirror. When I was seven, I asked him why he did it. He looked down at me, him in nothing but his boxers, a gut like a sack spilling over two fishing poles, a cigarette reduced to a limb of ash hanging from his lip, an empty bottle of something by the faucet, and I knew then nothing this guy said was ever going to pretty-up his ashtrays, stained teeth, and bad breath. Nothing he said was going to pretty-up my father.

He put out his cigarette in the sink and let its filter gather with its fellow expats at the mouth of the drain. "It's art. Art has no meaning without death," he rasped, his breath between a campfire and Datu Puti spiced vinegar. Being a complete idiot-kid, I believed him. Art was gruff. Art was butts in the drain. Art was sour smells and pain. In other words, growing up, I always saw my father in league with the writers I later learned to admire, akin to Edgar Allan Poe or Ernest Hemingway or Hunter S. Thompson. Tough guys who dealt as much as they were given, for art's sake. My family library was filled with their books, standing just as closed and mute as my father.

But little did my father know, he wasn't going to drown in a puddle or bite the barrel of a gun or get his ashes shot out of a cannon by Edward Scissorhands. No, he didn't die with a cigarette in his mouth, poetically watching his own life go out in the mirror like a fading star hidden in the slow morning fog. When he died, he was alone, and none of us could see him or retrieve his body afterward. He went out for one last stroll in the night and never came back. Someone found him face down on the sidewalk just a block away from his home, called an ambulance, and saw him off. It was no one who cared about him or knew he was a writer.

Not many knew he wrote. He scribbled in notebooks he never showed anyone, read books he never talked about. My father's literary life was a private one, but it wasn't anything so virtuous as "art for art's sake." He wrote only to please himself, and when he was done with something, he would stare at it for hours at his writing desk before hiding it away. Whatever didn't work he tore from the page and burned in an ashtray.

When he died, my mother and I gathered all his notebooks and hard drives and laid them in an old Crock-Pot box. My dad's entire life's work fit into the former container of a cheap promotional item he received for applying for a casino card. We taped it up and locked it in the trunk of his old red '59 Chevy Bel Air along with its keys. The car was as good as a tomb, and the act was as close as we were ever going to get to a funeral.

"What do you think it's like?" I asked my mother as we stood before the car in the garage. We both held red plastic rosaries, about to begin Wednesday's Glorious Mysteries even though it was Thursday and should've been starting the Joyful ones. Quarantine made us all lose track of time. We didn't know when the "Resurrection of our Lord" ended and where "The Annunciation to Mary" began.

"Peaceful," she replied, already starting an "Our Father."

"No," I interrupted her, "I mean his writing. You ever read it before?"

"*Susmariosep! Hindi ko alam.* Only Jesus knows."

"He never read you anything? A story? A poem?"

"I thought we leave it alone, *na naman.* Let him rest, *anakong.*"

Not wanting to upset her, I didn't try to push my mother further about my father's writing and resigned myself to helping her bury it with our "Hail Marys" and "Glory Bes" and "Our Fathers" until there was nothing left to talk about.

Although I never saw my father's writing and respected him enough in life not to ask after it, he never stopped hounding me about mine. As soon as I could form a coherent story, he was already picking on my diction and syntax, correcting my grammar, omitting my adverbs, and striking a red pen through clunky sentences and unnecessary descriptions. His notes in the margins were the worst. Once, he simply wrote the word "*pangit*" in bold letters above the first page and nothing else. I had barely started fourth grade, but I already understood the irony of a commentator writing "ugly" in a different language from the one being critiqued. Pain was a universal language, and my father never let me forget it.

Thankfully, I deviated from the less lucrative career of literary fiction and chose the path of sports journalism for myself in college and never looked back. To my father, I was selling out. He said I had chosen "the dependable and unequivocally boring" side of writing. To him, there was nothing artistic in reporting stats and creating top-ten lists. He believed that I had chosen this path because I was afraid of "the arduous nature of the road not taken," but in all honesty, it was merely because I was afraid of "the arduous nature of the road taken with my father." In sports, I found a door to writing through which he couldn't follow. It was the first time I was free from his callous influence, and writing had finally become as liberating as it was supposed to be.

Add this to my moving to Los Angeles to write basketball columns while they stayed in San Diego and one could determine the reasons why my father and I eventually stopped talking altogether. He despised sports and didn't even know what dribbling meant. What was there to talk about?

Don't get me wrong; I loved my father, and I can honestly tell you I tried to connect with him in other ways, but though writing fiction had been the one bond we had, I severed it with no regrets. I couldn't stand any more of the one-sided assaults on my words and ego. I set my roots where he couldn't touch me, and now it was his turn to reap what he couldn't sow. He didn't have anyone else to talk to about writing. All the other writers he knew were dead or didn't take emails. Alone, he retreated further into himself, sulking and growling like a child whenever I was on the line with my mother.

My father missed me, but his pride wouldn't allow him to back down. Once, my mother suggested my father visit me in Los Angeles by himself. "Bonding-bonding," she called it, although there was nothing left to bond over.

"Your *tatay* wants to *pasyal*, let him *pumunta doon*," she said, only the top of her head showing in the FaceTime call. My father was nowhere around.

"And why aren't you coming, Ma?"

"You boys need boys' talk. *Dati ka* talk and talk. How come no more? *Usap ng usap buong gabi.*"

"I think you confuse talking with arguing."

"*Nakong*, please. He really wants to go. It's good for you. *Sige na, ha?*"

I imagined my poor mother on the other side trying to convince my father I was the one inviting him, and I couldn't help but pity her. "What is he going to do here? I'm working," I stated, although my job really allowed me to work from anywhere there was a TV and/or an internet connection.

"Doesn't matter *ang gagawin*! Bonding-bonding *na!*"

Before long, my father arrived at LAX and we began our "bonding-bonding" with an awkward hug and a quiet car ride to my apartment in Eagle Rock. It was the day of Kobe Bryant's last game and I had the radio on to the sports station to gather what everyone's thoughts were about how he would go out. It was one of the most anticipated nights in sports history. Kobe's farewell season had been a dismal one, but his last game was the hottest ticket in town. Every sports journalist was vying for a press pass, but I didn't even try. My column didn't require I physically be there, and besides, I had my father to entertain.

My father looked out the window and occasionally picked out a small pad of paper and a black pen from his breast pocket to jot something down before tucking them away. I could tell he wasn't listening to the talk. There was a story going on behind his eyes. It was like he wasn't even there.

"Dad, I have to watch Kobe's last game," I mentioned without looking over. We were already off the freeway and stopped at a red light a few miles from my apartment.

My father continued to look out the window. In the car beside him, a woman was tapping her fingers on her steering wheel, but I knew he didn't notice it. The radio mentioned there would be a complementary Kobe jersey for each person attending the game. "He still plays? Didn't he get injured?"

I nearly let my foot off the brake upon hearing his response. "Wow. You know about that?"

"Everybody knows about that."

"Yeah. Tore his Achilles. Was supposed to be a career ender but he came back."

"Amazing," he said, but I couldn't tell if he was serious about it or not.

"Well, you see why I need to watch it."

"Your *nanay* said you had to work."

"This is work."

He scoffed, baring his teeth. I remembered that look from whenever I tried to rebut one of his corrections.

The light turned green and our car went. "When we get to the apartment, we'll drop your bags then head to a gastropub for some food and the game. How's that sound?"

"Will it be loud?"

"It's Kobe's last game. There are probably going to be tons of people there. You want to order in instead?"

"Whatever you want to do." And I knew, when he said that, it meant he thought I was making a mistake, but I was just as stubborn as he was in getting my way.

When we arrived at the gastropub, Magic Johnson was recounting the contributions Kobe made to the Lakers organization and the NBA. His voice echoed loudly from the speakers while everyone watched. To my surprise, there was only a handful of people at the bar, but most of them were wearing a Kobe jersey. Some were wearing his number 8 while others wore his number 24. We sat ourselves at a booth and watched as Shaquille O'Neal came onto a big screen to welcome Kobe to his new life of retirement.

My father watched the screen across from me as Derek Fisher followed Shaq, then Phil Jackson, then Jack Nicholson in congratulating him. My father had retired from forty years of working at a medical supply company before I left for college, but there wasn't any sort of celebration. One day, he just stopped going to work and that was it. He was never really one for pageantry.

As Lawrence Tanter closed the ceremony before the game, the waitress came over and took our orders. By the time our drinks arrived, he was announcing Kobe's name in the line-up one last time. By the time our food arrived, Kobe had already missed his first five shots.

"Shouldn't you be taking notes?" my father said, sipping his beer. He had barely touched it.

"I get all the stats on my phone." I tapped my phone with my fork. It was opened to the in-game stat sheet.

"*Talaga.* That is convenient," he said, picking up his burger. Before he could take a bite, Kobe blocked Trevor Booker on the board and was rushing down to the other side of the court. The gastropub erupted in cheers. My father watched the screen and murmured something as Kobe split two defenders and made his first basket of the night. Everyone at the bar high-fived each other as they showed the replay.

"What did you say, Dad?" I asked, watching the tally turn to one block and a 1-out-of-6 field goal percentage.

"Who are they facing?"

"The Jazz," I said, cutting into my chicken marsala.

"The Jazz," he repeated and proceeded to put down his burger and write something in his notepad.

I pretended to eat while trying to get a glimpse at what he was writing, but my father's handwriting looked like it had been made by the frantic hand of a seismograph. As he wrote, another cheer came at another basket. The tally rose to 2 out of 7.

He put his notepad away and started eating. We ate in silence as the game continued. By the end of the first half, Kobe had twenty points with a 7-out-of-20 field goal percentage. The game was at 57–42, Jazz. Another video string of well-wishing players, coaches, and celebrities came on to bid him farewell.

My father finished his second beer. By then, we were already finished with our meals. "Well, that's it. Not bad for someone on the way out. Twenty points. Is that a lot?"

I was on the beginning of my second bourbon on the rocks and winced at the taste. I didn't ask for a specific kind and regretted it. "Twenty points isn't a lot for Kobe Bryant."

"C'est la vie," my father said and raised his hand to wave down our server. "Let's go. Just down that. I got the bill. My treat."

"Dad, the game's not over."

He looked at me and then continued to wave. "I know. I'm just tired. Can't you continue the game at home?"

I knew he had really believed the game ended at the second quarter, but I didn't see a point in correcting him like he did me my entire life. Instead, I looked him in the eye and downed my drink to let him know I knew he was wrong. The cheap alcohol went straight to my head, and by the time we got to the car, I knew I couldn't drive. I turned on the radio to the game, but my father reached over and turned the dial down.

"Listening to talk doesn't sober you up, *nakong*." My father laughed. He was amused by my drunkenness, but he too was flushed red and gleaming in the evening light. I had seen him drunk many times, but this was the first time we were drunk together.

"What sobers you up?" I asked, expecting his answer to be his cigarettes and drunken night walks, but he smiled and he did something I never heard him do before. He began to sing.

At first, I thought he was merely slurring in Tagalog, but as it continued, the words followed each other in a rolling rhythm. A stream of steady words flowed into a natural climbing chorus he kept surprisingly in key. At the end of the chorus, he smiled quietly in the glow of my radio light and the hum of my engine.

"What was that?"

"You sing *nakong.*"

"What?"

"You sing and it'll sober you up."

"I'm not that drunk."

"*Sus, nakong, nanaman.* It's easy. You watch," he said and repeated a couple lines of the first verse. "Now, you try."

"No, it's all in Tagalog, Dad. I don't even know what it means."

"*Aye, matigas ang ulo!* You don't need to know what it means. You just do it." His eyes were open now. He was pointing ahead of himself with his lips, humming.

"What is that song?"

"It's one of my favorites. It is a song about giving a gift. *Ang handugon.*"

"Do you sing a lot?"

"Only when I need to sober up. *Aking Kaibigan*. Only with friends."

I thought of all the times I found him drunk. He never sang and, save my mother and I who had to clean up after him, I didn't know he had any friends besides his books. He was always alone.

"Never heard you sing before. You're pretty good."

My father huffed. "It's nothing. Singing's nothing. It's just something that sounds pretty while you wait."

I imagined him singing in his car or in front of the bathroom mirror or on his walks, but it was hard for me to imagine him singing with other people. "Where'd you learn?"

He huffed again. "Learn? I didn't learn how to do it. I'm just repeating what I heard. I'm just repeating a message." He effortlessly sang a line again. "There. *Tignan?* I am just repeating, repeating. I'm not really saying or doing anything."

"Ok, well, you repeat things very well," I said, concentrating on the low hum of the engine in the car, the flow of the air from the vents. I closed my eyes and tried to sober up enough to get us back home.

"Are you going to sing now, *nakong*?"

"No. I'm just going to rest a bit and wait for this to pass. I can't sing like you, Dad. I don't work that way."

My father didn't say anything, but I could tell he was disappointed I didn't take his advice. That night, Kobe Bryant ended his career with sixty points. An amazing way for anyone to go out. I wrote about how he defied the odds and whatever expectations anyone had for him. Before the game, Shaquille O'Neil joked with him about scoring fifty points. He did that, added ten more points to it, and stole the win from the Jazz. It was a fairy-tale ending to his career.

Several years later, when Kobe died in Calabasas in a tragic helicopter crash along with his daughter and several others, my father tried to call me. I don't remember why I didn't pick up, but I never called him back about what he wanted. The whole world mourned Kobe's death. Everyone wrote about it. My father was the last thing on my mind.

Then, a couple of months after that, when my father died and all sports were canceled and the entire world was suffering through a pandemic, I found my thoughts returning to what my father tried to share with me. My mother never heard my father sing and, even when I recounted what happened during his visit, she still didn't believe that he ever could.

"I know your *tatay, nakong*. He did not sing," the top of her head said on FaceTime, alone in their home now as I was alone in mine.

"Ma, he did. He was surprisingly good."

"*Ano ang* song? What did he sing?"

"I don't know. A Tagalog song."

"*Ang* Tagalog song?"

"Yeah, about someone giving a gift."

"I don't know. Sing it and *sasabihin ko sayo*. I will try to see if I know it."

I tried to hum a little of what I remembered, but the words couldn't reach us. No matter how close we thought we came to finding them, we were always too far from what they were. Soon the humming lost all meaning. They weren't my father's words, they were mine.

Carabao

The way I'll always remember it is with Lolo's ring.

I had just learned from a TV show that it was possible to burn things with a magnifying glass if you angled it just right in the sun. I was in the backyard trying to burn holes into page nineteen of *Across Five Aprils* from my sixth-grade summer reading list when there was a knock from the inside of the sliding door to my lolo's room. It wasn't the backhand thud of his leathery knuckle I was accustomed to. Instead, it was the rattle of something more delicate.

I closed my book on my magnifying glass when I took my first look at her. Her skin was pale and rough like chalk. Her lips were a bright red gash across her face. She held her hands down at her stomach, my lola's old one-piece house dress that she had to tie at the shoulders when she was still alive, hugging the broad muscles and wide girth of this new woman's form. Even though it was my first time seeing her this way, I knew who she was and who she was supposed to be.

And when the sliding door opened, the ring of my lolo's old carabao bell around her neck—an old, repurposed glass bottle with three green *sunka* marbles in it—ushered the familiar fragrance of baby oil and calamansi face cleanser of a mature Filipina. She extended a freshly painted toe out to kiss the end of the doorway, an old smile on her face.

"Come inside *na, balong*," she said with my lolo's voice, not even trying to hide it, before stepping back in and walking away.

Before this, of course, there were things I didn't know or think much about as an eleven-year-old Filipino American boy in 1998. When most people were focused on Bill Clinton and Monica Lewinsky, I was studying GameFAQs about how to capture all 151 Pokemon in *Pokemon Red* and *Blue*. While the world celebrated the triumph of the Belfast Agreement, I was celebrating the sacrifice made by Bruce Willis in *Armageddon*. The closest thing that I got to an education on gender constructs was from comparing Jack to Rose in *Titanic*, Celine Dion to Metallica, Michael to Janet Jackson. No one ever had the talk with me either. I guess my family and my teachers and the rest of society just assumed someone else would teach me about it. That, or I'd just figure it out on my own.

And, I guess, this was one of those things my lolo expected my dad to have gotten used to after living here in the United States, especially in Los Angeles with its Hollywood and Beverly Hills and Downtown, for a little over fifteen years by then. But my dad grew up watching my lolo work in construction all his life. He watched my lolo lift heavy timbers and bend bamboo. He watched my lolo kill chickens and goats and pigs with bare hands. He watched my lolo lift his mother's casket on calloused shoulders and not shed a single tear. To my dad, my lolo was the epitome of what a man should be. But, there my lolo was now, not.

I had missed whatever storm occurred inside by the time my lolo called me in. My dad sat at the kitchen table, a forty-ounce of Red Horse opened but still full, warm. He was still stunned. How could he explain how he had just lost his father? How could he explain how he still was his son, me, his *apo*, his grandson?

"*Balong*," he started, but his mouth stopped moving, as if the words he was chewing on had suddenly turned to stone.

I gripped *Across Five Aprils*, the magnifying glass wedged where the pages were burnt. I recalled how some of the copies had been vandalized over the years. On their covers, the main character was penned over with an eyepatch or a beard, scars or horns. Not once did they draw long hair or blushed cheeks, a flowy dress or slender legs.

"*Balong*," my dad started again. He was a big man like my lolo was, towering over me even when he was sitting down, even when he was this low. "I need to tell you about your lolo before he comes back."

I sat down beside him, and he explained, as best as he could, how some men can change, even men like my lolo. How sometimes men can become women, how women can become men. How even though some things change, other things still stay the same.

However, I already learned from school that when you called a boy a girl or a girl a boy, it was nothing but an insult. To hear otherwise, let alone think otherwise, was too much for me to follow. And, based on how much his face twisted and his smile trembled, it was too much for my dad too. I started to feel my stomach turn and my head pound with the more he talked. It was easier not to have this conversation. It was easier for things to stay the same, to go back to normal.

Finally, my dad leaned forward and asked, "Are you sad?"

My head was still spinning. I tried to remember what I read that day, what I ate or the cartoon I watched that morning, but it was completely blank. It had been replaced by the pale figure standing in my lolo's doorway. I didn't care, I thought, but I did. I wanted to say something, but I didn't.

My shoulders rose and fell into a shrug.

"Well, don't be sad," my dad said, speaking more to himself than to me, and patted my arm. "Just because he's changed doesn't mean Lolo loves you any less than before." And this much we knew was true. But my father took a long time swallowing what was in his throat before he continued, "I mean Lola. Call her Lola."

I nodded but all I could think about was what the kids at school would say if they knew, all the ways I could keep everyone else from knowing. I felt like I did when I lost my two front teeth. I wished that I could hide Lolo with my hands. I wished that I could keep my mouth closed forever.

It wasn't until dinner when the familiar sound of Lolo's carabao bell bellowed from the hall. It used to hang on my lolo's knob across from the door to my room, and it would knock and chime each time the door opened and closed.

My lolo didn't start wearing it until that day I saw her, but I knew it had something to do with a story he told me the year before. I had twisted my ankle in the backyard and, stunned by the pain, I cried out, unable to move. Moments later, my lolo, still my lolo, emerged from his sliding door, scooped me up, wiped my tears with his *sando*, and gently placed me down on his bed.

"I'm fine," I said, biting back tears. I wanted to look strong in front of my lolo. If my lolo didn't cry, neither should I, I thought. "Lolo, you didn't have to."

"*Walang problema, balong.* I'm here," he said, sliding a pillow under my leg. "*Kukuha ako ng yelo.* I will get ice *ngayon.*"

"No, stay," I whimpered. "I don't need it. I don't want to be alone."

"*Nakakatawang bata.* Nothing will hurt you. You're safe. You just hurt yourself."

"Then I don't want to be alone with myself," I said, pulling at his shirt. I thought that if my lolo was close enough, what he was would somehow rub off on me. On *Power Rangers*, all they had to do was pass a coin to someone else. Surely my lolo would do something like that, I thought, surely he would give me his strength one day.

"You're afraid you'll hurt yourself? *Aye, susmariosep.* It won't make it good. It won't make your leg better, *na.*"

"Please, Lolo."

"What do I do then? What do you want?"

"Just stay here, Lolo."

"*Aye,*" he said and stayed. He sat beside me on the other side of the bed. "Everyone gets hurt, *balong.*"

"No, not you! You never get hurt."

My lolo smiled down and patted my leg before facing forward and crossing his arms. He leaned back on his headboard, looking up at the altar nailed on the wall above his television. I used the think the tiny Santo Niño there was just a fancy girl's doll, and he never told me otherwise. I had to learn on my own that it was supposed to be God.

"That's true now. But when I was small, *maliit*, like you, I got hurt all the time. *Sa buong panahon.*"

"Who hurt you? I'll hurt them back, Lolo. We can get them. Dad, you, and me," I said, and I felt the blood rush to my heart, almost forgetting about my ankle, until its warm heat buzzed through my leg and up my spine.

My lolo laughed and put his arm around me. "I mostly hurt myself too. You want to fight your lolo?" He squeezed and shook my shoulders, the weight of his full power dulled by his playfulness.

I shook my head, leaning into him. I used to imagine that I was one of only a few safe in his arms, that if it was anyone other than Lola or Dad or me, he would've wrung the life out of them.

"When I was small, my *tatay*, your, *paano ko sasbihin*? Your, uh, *great*-lolo, would hit me with *isang latigo*, a bullwhip."

"Why, Lolo?" I said thinking about Zorro and Indiana Jones. I could hear their whips slash through the air, I could feel their crack and snap.

"Your great-lolo didn't like things your Lolo would do sometimes. Sometimes your lolo deserved it. Sometimes your lolo didn't. But every time, *aray ko! Masakit!* It hurt. I would have *sugat* on my arms, *sugat* on my legs, *sugat* on my back, my hands, my head. *Sobrang sakit nila*, they would hurt so much I couldn't sleep. I would run away from him, I would hide, *Magtatago ako*. But your great-lolo's whip would always find me."

I studied my lolo's arms and legs and one after another, they appeared. The bites of his father's whip covered his body like white hairs, like the ghosts of tiny snakes. Had he never mentioned them, I would have never noticed. My lolo could hide things in plain sight. My lolo could hide things without trying, and even without meaning to sometimes.

I traced a line at his collar with my eyes, another at his chin, above his brow, below his left eye. "Do they still hurt, Lolo?"

My lolo studied me as if I was one of his scars. "They used to. Not anymore. *Sa katapusan*, I learned how not to let the whip of your great-lolo hurt me."

"What did you do?"

My lolo looked me over again and then he looked across me, out his door to the hall. "Well, your lolo turned into a carabao."

"A carabao?"

"A carabao."

At the time, I had never seen a carabao in real life. I had only seen ones in pictures from my titas and titos who still worked the land in the province where my lolo and my dad were from. In one picture, a tito is holding onto the creature's tail while it pulls him and a bedframe-turned-till behind it with ropes fastened to its horns. In another, three of my young cousins ride on its back, flashing peace signs and middle fingers, flaunting smiles with missing teeth. In both pictures, the carabao looks off, a dull glaze in its eyes.

"Why?" I asked. I didn't understand why my lolo wanted to be anyone other than who he was.

"*Amerikano ka*. You were born here, so you don't know, *balong*. The carabao is the national symbol of the Filipino. It's hardworking. It's patient. It's loyal. It gets things done. It's a real blessing in the sky, *na*."

"Don't you mean blessing in disguise?"

"It's a Filipino saying, but it means the same thing, *balong*. One day, I was hiding in the *palayan* when I heard this clinking-clinking. I was like, *ano iyon*? What was that? When I heard the clinking-clinking get closer, I peek over the *damo*, the tall grass, and I see it: *ang pinakamalaking* carabao, the biggest carabao I ever seen in my life. It was pulling a tiny cart with a tiny farmer in it. Around the carabao's thick neck was a bottle with three marbles clinking-clinking inside as it moved. The farmer was whipping it to go faster but it didn't mind. It didn't feel pain, *balong*, no matter how many times the farmer hit it. It just went faster and faster. *Napakabilis!* After seeing that, I knew that's what I wanted to be. *Kaya*, the next time my *tatay* and his whip came after me, I got a bottle, put some marbles in it, fastened *isang lubid*, a rope, and wore it around my neck. As soon as the whip hit me, *nagbago ako*. I changed."

The woman my lolo became emerged from her room. Still in her wife's old dress, she moved how I never thought my lolo could. Her hips swayed from left to right while her arms stayed straight down at her sides, her hands fanned out and tipping up and down with each step she took. On her face was the same bloodred lipstick from that afternoon, except now it was accompanied by black eyeliner, eyebrows filled in and curved with pencil, and my lolo's balding head.

I mashed my dad's canned corned beef and sautéed onions and garlic fried rice together with my fork, trying to build up an appetite but I couldn't. I hated myself for hating her, but I did. I couldn't forgive her for what she did to Dad, me, and Lolo.

My dad got up when he saw her. It had been years since my mother and my lola died, years since a woman had lived in the house. Now that there was one again, my dad didn't know how to act.

"*Nanay*," he said and stood up straight. It was strange to hear my dad call Lolo anything other than *Tatay* or his father.

I looked at both of them standing together. Lolo was easily still the biggest and strongest of them. I used to stay up at night imagining the three of us going on adventures like in *Mighty Max* or *Johnny Quest*. My father and I were the same, but Lolo, he always changed, he was always the muscle. He was our Norman and Race. He was the one who was always there when the going got tough.

Lolo's burly arm extended to me. If it wanted to, it could have strangled a snake, it could have brandished a sword. Instead, it hung limp, each of her fingernails meticulously painted with glitter, shimmering in the dying light peeking through the window.

"*Balong*," my dad said. "*Mano* your Lola."

"Lola," I said, and took her hand. Hearing my dad call her Lola and ask me to do the same felt like a betrayal. As if Lolo was so easy to let go after all he had done for us. His grip, once strong, was so loose, so soft. Although it was twice the size of mine, it felt like I wasn't holding anything at all. All of Lolo's power was lost. Only her touch remained.

"*Balong*," Lolo said, something lost in her voice as if it were coming from far away. I only thought about what it meant to *mano* someone when I finally pressed her hand to my forehead, and immediately regretted it. It was supposed to be a sign of respect, but how could I respect someone who had left me? How could I respect a stranger?

The next couple of months were not kind to any of us. My lolo left, mostly because we didn't stop her. She moved into a trailer park and a one-bedroom mobile home down the street. Everything of my lolo's emptied out of our house in a mere matter of days. While we loaded my dad's car, it was easy for me to avoid my lolo because of the ring of the carabao bell around her neck. By the time she left for good, we only spoke twice. Once, to ask if she was ready to go, the second time to say goodbye.

By the time I got back to school, I hadn't made any progress with *Across Five Aprils*. I took to burning holes into my math sheets with my magnifying glass by day, playing *Pokemon Red* and falling asleep to the music of Pallet Town by night. My dad never asked how I was, and he never asked me to come with him whenever he visited my lolo. After school, I would wait on campus until his visit was over. The first month of the semester came and went, and I was failing all my classes, my dad ignoring the calls from my teachers, signing the progress reports without reading them.

Then in October, my dad lost his job. He wasn't worried, but he said it would take time for him to find another. In the meantime, there would be sacrifices. When he scheduled his first interview, he picked me up from school and there was no time to fix the wobble in his throat before he said he would be dropping me off to stay with my lolo for a couple of hours.

"Just a couple of hours, *balong*," he said, pretending to concentrate on the traffic.

By then, I had not seen my lolo in a little over two months. It was difficult to remember her from before without thinking about who she was now. I nodded, even though I knew he couldn't see me.

"*Balong?*" my father said, squeezing his wheel. It was tiny in his hands, but in that moment, he looked so small.

"I'm fine with it," I said, although I wasn't and I wouldn't be. But I understood sacrifice. I understood that in my dad's and my lolo's absence, I needed to be the man.

When we got to my lolo's trailer, my dad let me out and drove off, leaving me to meet my lolo at her door alone. Although

it wasn't my first time there, it had been my first time seeing it after she had fully settled in. The tiny wooden steps to
the landing were draped in the black rubber runners my lolo
used to keep on the steps down to our yard, now a little less
than completely ruined by the rain. My lolo cut them from
rolls and fastened them down in places he knew I was sure to
slip and fall. After my lolo left, I barely went outside, and the
yard was untamed, wild, and a world apart.

At the door, my lolo met me in a new house dress. It was
bright brown with white patterns of grass rising up her right
hip and sagging at her left shoulder. It was none of the ones
Lola had worn before she died, none of the ones Lolo had
worn before she left. Besides the dress, she was still bald, still
covered in makeup from head to toe and smelling like baby
oil and calamansi, still wearing Lolo's carabao bell like I last
saw her, but there was also something else. Her makeup no
longer caked on her face, the lipstick blended with her lips,
and her smell was stronger than before: less like my lolo,
more like my lola.

She took me in close and I closed my eyes and let her reach
her huge arms around me. When she squeezed, my face sunk
into the familiar cushion of my lolo's stomach. In the dark
warmth of it, I gripped my backpack, trying to keep myself
from reaching out to find my lolo hiding somewhere in there,
to wrap my arms around my lolo's vast form, to shake the
glass bottle of the carabao bell to my ear.

"*Matagal na hindi nakikita, balong.* Long time no see!" Her nose buried in the top of my head, breathing me in. To my surprise, her voice was still my lolo's.

She let go, and I felt my muscles relax from the strain. I nodded and let go of the straps of my backpack. I felt the indentations they made with my closed fists, the cold kiss of her glass carabao bell fresh on my cheek, as I waited for her to let me in.

The jubilation in her face made me happier than I thought I would be, but still, I tried to bury it and squeezed past her in the doorframe before I could *mano* her, before I could give her my respect.

"*Aye, pasok ka.* You must be hungry. I have *merienda* on the table. Some *itlog at* Vienna sausage."

She closed the door, her bell ringing after me. The floor was thin carpet that seemed to shake with each of our steps. At the far end was the kitchen and the door to her bedroom. Closest to me was her dining table and a couple of chairs. To my left was her couch and the television talking about the space shuttle Discovery launch.

I plunged into the couch and hugged my backpack. I closed my eyes, hoping to fall asleep and let time ebb away without much interaction, without conflict, but my lolo clinked into the seat beside me, her weight tilting me in her direction.

"How was school, *balong*?" she said, rubbing my back.

I softened at her touch, but I said nothing. I didn't want to feel comfortable with her. I didn't want her to feel comfortable with me.

For a while, her hand stayed on my shoulder and the news rolled from one item to another, Tom Hanks on *Saving Private Ryan*, an armed robbery, a high-speed chase, and the impending doom of the Y2K bug.

When it got back to the Discovery launch, I was still wide awake, feeling the couch tremble with each of Lolo's resting breaths, the static crunching in my ears, slowly rising from the silence.

Then, finally, my lolo spoke, "You hear about the space-shut Discovery, *balong*?"

I couldn't help myself from laughing. "Spaceship, Lolo," I said and opened my eyes to her.

"*Aye, Tanga*. Space shuttle Discovery," she said, patting my shoulder, not correcting my calling her Lolo.

"We learned about it today in science," I said, looking at the screen as they prepared for launch. People were gathered before the ship while a small screen showed the astronauts settling in, their puffy orange suits brushing the instruments. I kept my eyes on each buckle they fastened, the kind of sunglasses the spectators wore, the color of Bill Clinton's tie, Hillary Clinton's dress. Anything to keep myself from looking over at my lolo.

"That John Glenn is seventy, *balong*. Seventy like your lolo. *Matanda na siya*," she said as if she weren't referring to herself.

I watched as a man in white helped prop John Glenn into his seat. Despite his age, he was able to pull himself up, the man helping him barely touching him, hugging his form like a shadow. It was not hard to see the two of them as one and the same, my lolo and this astronaut.

For the next hour, we watched the newscasters report the flight. They talked about their mission, the specs of the ship, and John Glenn's personal life and career leading up to the launch. At one point, a plane came too close to the launch and caused a delay. Every other reporter was calling the event John Glenn's historic return to space. To me, it was the first time seeing something not a movie get so much attention. To me, it was the first time seeing the real thing and feeling the real power and fear that comes from something so massive. It wasn't anything like the high drama in *Armageddon*. It wasn't anything like the graceful ballet of cartoon spaceships transforming into fighting robots.

At thirty seconds, when the ship's computers took automatic control, I found myself sunk into my lolo, her arm around me, holding me tight, Lolo's carabao bell between us, shaking, ringing. Before I could think of getting away, the tally ran out, and at the announcement of booster ignition, smoke plumed in all directions and two screaming pillars of light lifted the rocket up into the blue-gray fuzz on screen.

The TV and the house and the space between us rang with sound and the ship tilted into the sky for a full two minutes before the shuttle's twin-rocket booster burned out and separated, letting Discovery go on its own way, shrinking to a quiet, singular dot, then nothing. Mission control continued to rattle off "systems nominal" as the television cut between crowds cheering across the country. My lolo and I sunk into each other.

"Wow. *Balong!* Did you see that?" I felt the familiar shake of my lolo's arms, the singing of her carabao bell, and I couldn't help but smile back. Among the scientific jargon and mission reports and the scientists and reporters and spectators and astronauts, there was a team on a mission riding on a behemoth force like a carabao going at full speed.

The Discovery still had much left to its journey, but this wouldn't be the last we saw of it. One day, it would return. One day, it would land.

Biographical Note

E. P. Tuazon is a Filipino American writer from Los Angeles. They have work in several publications such as *The Rumpus*, *Lunch Ticket*, *Peatsmoke*, and *Five South*. Their work was chosen by ZZ Packer as the winner of the 2022 AWP Grace Paley Prize in Short Fiction. They are currently a member of Advintage Press and The Blank Page Writing Club at The Open Book, Canyon Country. In their spare time, they like to go to Filipino seafood markets to gossip with the crabs.